THE PLUS ONES

USA TODAY BESTSELLING AUTHOR

Kayley Loring

THE PLUS ONES

KAYLEY LORING

2023 COVER DESIGNER: Najla Qamber Designs
COPY EDITOR: Jenny Rarden

To the readers, bloggers, Facebookers and
bookstagrammers
who email, message, mention and tag me.
Thank you for reminding me why it's totally worth it to sit
on my pale ass in front of a computer all day in my office,
instead of lying on a beach in the Caribbean...

KILIG:

A feeling of exhilaration or elation caused by an exciting or romantic experience.

-- Oxford English Dictionary definition of the Tagalog word

The feeling of butterflies in your stomach, usually when something romantic or cute takes place.

-- LOST IN TRANSLATION definition by Ella Frances Sanders

Literally what I live for.

-- Kayley Loring

PROLOGUE - ROXY

* Chase and Aimee's Wedding *
Five Years Ago

Keaton *fucking Bridges.*

Look at him, all handsome and sweet over there, in that bespoke three-piece suit with that silver tie and his quivering voice. I'd almost like him if I didn't hate him so much for giving a better toast than I did. I crushed it! But he's killing it.

Okay, maybe my Maid of Honor speech was a tad on the overly emotional cheeseball side. Maybe I should have come better prepared. Perhaps I should have waited until *after* my toast to indulge in five glasses of champagne. But my best friend and former roommate is getting married to the love of her life. While pregnant. Things are changing. How else am I supposed to cope?

I didn't even bring a date to this wedding. I couldn't think of one guy I wanted to share this special night with. It's weird that Keaton didn't bring a date either.

Or not. Maybe it's not weird. I mean, he did get his heart broken a few months ago. He probably isn't over his ex-girlfriend yet. That's probably why he's so choked-up tonight.

"I've known Chase since we were in college," Keaton says into the mic, "and he's always been the guy everyone wanted to be around, the guy who made me a better person. But when he and Aimee are together, they become this metaphorical third thing that's better than anything I've ever witnessed. They've created an awesome new home together, a successful new company, and now..." He pauses to clear his throat. Goddammit, his eyes are tearing up.

"Now they're creating an actual third person for all of us to love, and I want you both to know that I will do anything I can for you and your family, always." He looks down at Chase and grins at him. "You complete me. And she completes you. I love you, man."

Fucking. Hell.

That was perfect.

That was the *best* Best Man toast I have ever heard.

He is so getting laid tonight.

Not by me.

Obviously.

I can't stand him.

Mr. Hoity Toity Pretty Boy, my dad would call him.

Look at him over there. Doing a group hug with Chase and Aimee.

I'll bet he thinks he's their favorite.

He's not the favorite.

I'm the favorite.

I'm the one who was never an immature, rich, entitled ass.

I'm the one who wasn't a little shit to them two years ago when they first got together. Just because he wanted to date Aimee. He was such a dick!

He may have changed, but some of us don't have to change.

Okay, maybe I should stop swearing so much if I'm going to be around Aimee's kid once she has it.

But *I'm* the *best* best friend.

I'm the one who'd really do anything for Aimee and Chase and their future spawn.

Where's Roxy's group hug?

And where's that waiter with my champagne refill?

"Roxy!" I hear Aimee call out. "Get in on this!" She waves me over to join the group hug.

I roll my eyes at her, even though I know that she knows that I am dying to get in on that. I get up slowly and trudge over to join Aimee, Chase, and Keaton fucking Bridges in an absolutely epic embrace. It's fucking beautiful. God, we're a bunch of cornballs tonight. If I didn't love us so much, I'd be making fun of us so hard. If I weren't so focused on how happy I am for my best friend, I'd knee Keaton in the balls for putting his hand on my waist like this.

I've never been this close to him before. It's almost creepy how chiseled his jawline is. It is genuinely annoying how good he smells. Like the Barney's men's grooming and fragrance department. He smells like the opposite of my type.

"I feel like maybe we've hugged long enough now," Chase mutters, but he waits for his bride to confirm and end the hug.

"Wrap it up, Gilpin," I say and then immediately realize she's a McKay now. "I mean—wrap it up, Mrs. McKay."

"That's more like it," Chase grumbles, but he can't stop smiling.

So fucking cute.

When Aimee and Chase drop their arms, Keaton slowly removes his hand from my waist, his fingers accidentally grazing my ass. If Aimee weren't putting one hand on each of our faces and squeezing our cheeks, I would totally call him on it.

"I love you guys so much. Thank you for your beautiful speeches." She kisses Keaton on the cheek and then kisses me on the cheek, and then she and Chase get pulled away by relatives, and Keaton and I are left standing here.

He nods at me. "Roxy."

I roll my eyes—which is a mistake because it almost shakes a tear loose. "Keaton. Those are some friendly fingers you've got on you tonight."

He winks and straightens his tie with those fingers. "If you'd like them on *you* tonight, just let me know."

That's what I thought.

But there's something...something about the way he looks at me that hints that he's not just being a cocky flirt. It makes me...step back and walk away.

I pass Aimee's cousin, one of the bridesmaids, on my way to the ladies' room. We smile and nod at each other. I overhear her telling her friend that she's going to "go get me some of that Best Man now."

You go, girl. Good luck with that.

I'm gonna go cry in a bathroom stall like a proper Maid of Honor.

Okay, I could not cry in the bathroom stall because there were so many women waiting in line. Fucking Green-point event loft with *one* bathroom stall in the ladies room. Where's a girl gotta go to weep with a little dignity around here?

The dancing portion of the evening has begun, and I refuse to stand around with this tingling nose and these eyes that sting and this lump in my throat.

I look out the glass doors to the deck. Surprisingly, it appears to be empty. Everyone's inside dancing and being all happy and coupled-up. No one will notice if Foxy Roxy disappears out there for two minutes to squeeze a few drops of this stupid burning liquid from my tear ducts. I don't make eye contact with anyone as I head for the doors.

As soon as I step out into the night and breathe that fresh air, I feel better.

This loft is on the third floor, and there's a view of the East River with the Manhattan skyline beyond.

I walk straight over to the railing and stand in a dark corner, facing the river, and let my stupid inner crybaby do her thing.

Fucking weddings.

I let out a loud sigh, grab on to the railing and let my head drop back, squeezing my eyes shut.

"Are you crying?"

I whip around, wiping the corners of my eyes with my fingertips.

Keaton fucking Bridges.

"Did you follow me out here?"

"I was here first. You just didn't see me." His hands are in his pockets. I don't know how anyone can look so casual in such an expensive suit, like he was born in it.

"Were *you* crying?"

"I was processing some emotions in a totally cool and masculine way, in private. Or so I thought."

"Well, don't let me stop you from processing. Ignore me."

"I think that would be impossible, Roxy Carter." His head is cocked to one side, and he's staring at me. Not grinning or smirking, not checking me out or flirting, just...regarding me.

I can't handle it.

Maybe if I were in my usual Foxy Roxy attire, but not tonight. Not in this pretty lavender spaghetti-strap dress that I would only ever wear for my favorite girl in the world. Not with my hair up and my neck exposed.

Everything about me feels exposed right now.

I narrow my eyes at him. "Screw you, Bridges."

And now he's smirking. And there's that dimple. That dimple that let him get away with being an immature, rich, entitled ass for so many years. "Can't take a compliment?"

"Is *that* what that was?"

He shifts on his heels and turns to face the view, turning his attention to the Upper East Side, where he grew up. "I liked your speech. It was sweet. You're a good friend," he says, not looking at me.

"Thanks for the feedback."

I hear air blow out of his nostrils. He's quietly laughing at me. Whatever, I'm not being defensive.

"I liked your speech too. It was very...*not you.*"

"Thanks. I guess."

We both look back toward the inside space when we hear Aimee's joyful shriek and loud laughter. Chase and Aimee are dancing, and he just dipped her—very carefully. Those guys. So cute.

"I really love those guys," Keaton says as we watch them together. A statement. Not even a cheesy one.

"Yeah. Me too."

"I can't believe I'm gonna be a godfather."

I snap my head around. "They told you they want you to be his godfather?"

He grins. "No. I'm just assuming. I'm sure they'll ask you to be the godmother."

"They fucking better."

"I have no fucking doubt you'll be the best fucking godmother ever."

"You better fucking believe I will." *Shit, I really need to stop swearing so much.*

"I do."

I do. Those two little words make me feel all giggly inside. At a wedding. Even when it's Keaton Bridges who's uttering them.

All of a sudden, I'm so aware of the fact that there's so much love and light inside there, so many of Chase and Aimee's family and friends and co-workers, and it's just Keaton and me out here. Outside, looking in. Everyone in our circle of friends is married now, besides us. Chase and Aimee. Matt and Bernadette. Vince and Nina. For a second it feels like this is how it's going to be from now on. Not him and me together, but...Him. And me. Apart. From them.

I shiver at the thought of it.

"You cold?" he asks.

It's a ridiculous question, even if he is being polite. It's a warm, humid summer night. But he looks down at me like he knows exactly what I was thinking. His brown eyes are sad, in a happy-sad kind of way, and it's killing me just a little bit.

"I'm fine," I whisper.

"You sure?"

I feel his hand touch my back, ever so slightly, and it makes me shiver in a completely different way.

"Yeah." I take a step away from him and turn to face the view again. "You wishing your ex was here tonight?"

"I guess." He turns back to face the view too. "I mean, I wish she wanted to be here. Y'know?"

I nod. "Yeah. Sorry." Surprisingly, I really am sorry for him. I liked her—Tamara. Aimee and Chase liked her. He obviously loved her. Aimee said he was devastated when she decided to move to LA without him. He would have moved there with her, but she just didn't want him to. It was over for her. And he was heartbroken. Still is, probably.

"You seeing anyone?"

I shrug my shoulders. "No one special. Y'know. You?"

He shakes his head. "Not at all."

Silence. There's music coming from inside. There's traffic noise and people out on the streets below us. But it just seems so quiet all of a sudden as I feel him eyeing me.

I clear my throat. "You should get back in there and talk to Aimee's cousin. She's been eye-boning you all night."

"Has she? I hadn't noticed."

I glance over at him, ever so quickly. He doesn't look away. It's not that I'm not comfortable being looked at. Or stared at. With a rack like mine and a mouth like the one I've got on me. I'm just not used to being looked at or stared at by him. He's not staring at my rack. He's not responding to some wisecrack I just made. He's just looking at me. And I'm definitely not comfortable with it.

In the good way.

In the tingly way.

Because he looks so handsome and he's being so sweet.

Two thoughts I've never had about Keaton Bridges before.

But he's got this vibe tonight... It's so...

And this all feels so...

It's that freaking Chainsmokers song that just came on. It's this beautiful summer night. It's all that champagne. All those wonderful people in there. That custom-made suit with that silver tie. These strings of warm white café lights all over the place that make everything feel so romantic. Everything... It's just messing with my head. Or my heart. Or my ovaries.

"Don't take this the wrong way," he says, looking out at the view again, "but you look really beautiful tonight. I just...wanted to make sure you know that."

I resist every urge to scoff at him or tell him to fuck off, and the strangest thing happens. I feel it. I feel the compliment, instead of just assuming he's saying it because he wants to fuck me. Because he doesn't. It's Keaton. He's just looking at me with those sad brown eyes, like...like he wants me to know that I look beautiful tonight. That he noticed. That he notices me.

"Thank you," I say, my voice barely a whisper.

He nods. "You're welcome." He turns back to look out at the river and exhales, like he's finally said what he wanted to say and there's nothing left to say anymore.

Except now I want him to keep talking.

Or I want him to...

What?

Make me feel less like I'm on the outside looking in.

Keep making me feel beautiful tonight.

And as if he just heard my thoughts, he twitches, takes one step toward me, pulls me in toward him with one hand, and places the other under my chin to lift it up as he kisses me. It all happens so fast I can't do anything other than hold his face and kiss him back. I can't do anything other than grab on to his lapels and respond to his lips and his tongue and his hands and the soft moans and the quickening of our breaths. I can't ignore what's going on between my legs and I really can't ignore what's pressing against my thigh.

I never would have pegged this guy for a good kisser, but holy shit.

I know what this is, though.

This kiss is a silent conversation between two not-exactly-friends, about loneliness and confusion and trying to hang on to something that was so good and now it's changing and we're happy and sad at the same time because what if that thing that those people have will never come for us?

This kiss is restrained and urgent and reassuring and alarming, and it is shaking me to my core.

When his lips find that spot high on my neck, below my earlobe, I groan and my knees give out.

My knees actually lose their ability to hold up the rest of my body.

He holds me tighter and lifts me up without pausing his gentle assault on my neck.

This is not the drunken make-out session of two reckless partygoers who just need to get through the night.

This is leading somewhere, and it is not somewhere either of us are meant to go to together. Not with each other. Not ever.

I push back against his hard chest, pull away from him.

He emits a low guttural sound, his eyelids heavy, but he complies.

I wipe my lip gloss from my chin and his, watching him as we both slow our breaths and straighten ourselves up and remember where we are and who we are and who we aren't to each other.

For all I know, he could have been thinking about his ex-girlfriend while he was kissing me.

"I'll go back inside first, okay?" I say. "You wait out here a couple of minutes."

He nods. His brown hair is always perfectly mussed-up in that way that only a two-hundred-dollar haircut and hair product can make it, but it is really mussed-up now. I shouldn't touch him again, but I have to run my fingers through his hair to make him look more presentable.

He wraps his long fingers around my wrist. Presses his lips against the palm of my hand very quickly. His eyes are less bleary now, but they are asking me a question.

Should we?

I want to laugh, because obviously we shouldn't. We couldn't. He's a grown-up trust fund kid. I will always be the daughter of a mechanic. Things are already so different between us and our best friends, and if we sleep together even once, it will just change things even more.

He knows this. It's not really him asking this; it's his boner. I'm no dummy. I know how boners work. I know how weddings work. I know how I work.

I pull my hand free from his soft grip, touch his cheek, and shake my head. "See you around, Bridges."

I walk away from him, away from the summer night air and the strings of warm white lights that are hanging overhead just for us and the most surprising kiss of my life and the guy that I have no doubt I will go back to wanting to dropkick the next time I see him.

I freaking hope.

CHAPTER 1
KEATON

* Matt and Bernie's Christmas Party *
Five Years Later

Roxy fucking Carter.

Of course she got here before me. Probably hoped she could leave before I got here, like she did last year. Like she's managed to do at least half the time at our friends' parties over the past five years. She tried to convince me to do a time-share when Aimee was having her baby at the hospital—because they didn't need both of us there at the same time. She tried to convince Chase and Aimee to have two separate birthday parties for Finn, every year, one for each godparent. Anytime our friends get together for brunch, she seats herself at the opposite end of the table from me and only talks to me when she's hurling some sassy one-liner at me from a safe distance.

Like I'm some stalker who's dying to get into her pants.

Get over yourself, blondie.

It was one kiss.

Five years ago.

It was one fucking awesome, hot, confusing kiss between two people who were caught up in the emotions of their best friends' wedding.

Get over it.

I did.

I haven't forgotten it, but I'm over it.

I've been busy working my ass off, making investments, making millions, traveling the world. Admittedly, there has been a lot more business than pleasure in my life lately, which makes the time pass quicker somehow. Admittedly, in those moments when I'm alone in a hotel room in Tokyo or Sydney or London and I can't get to sleep, my mind goes to that moment out on the deck in Greenpoint. To the way her hands gripped the lapels of my suit jacket and the way her tits pressed against my chest and the way she nibbled hungrily on my lower lip and moaned so quietly.

But that's just because it didn't go anywhere, so it's easier for my mind to fill in the blanks. I like the blanks. The blanks are what make it such a vivid memory. For me, anyway.

Clearly I rocked Foxy Roxy's world and the only way she thinks she can keep her balance is by avoiding me so it doesn't happen again.

It won't happen again.

It was a one-time thing.

It was the wedding. It was the champagne. It was the speeches and the group hug. It was the strings of warm white lights and the summer night air. It was knowing that things were changing and that we might not be ready for what our friends were experiencing. Whether we wanted it or not.

And yeah, sure, it was her fucking hot body in that dainty little dress and the way her hair was all piled up on her head and that exposed neck and the way she kissed me back like it was the only thing that mattered to her. Like that kiss could make time stand still. And it did. For a minute.

But if she needs to believe I'm still the rich dick I was when she met me, then I'm happy to play that part for her. No matter how small a role she wants me to play in her life.

Your loss, sweetheart.

Tonight, all I care about is seeing my friends and their kids. It's been way too long. Chase and Aimee spent Thanksgiving in Ann Arbor this year. Matt and Bernie were in Vermont. Vince and Nina were in Indiana. Their afternoons and weekends are usually spent shuttling their kids back and forth between activities. They all have kids the same age who go to the same preschool, so they see each other all the time. I've got my work friends, my buddies from school... It's not like I don't have anything to do. But it's not the same. These are the people I want to be around, right here.

"Hey, man." Matt McGovern's voice startles me so much, I actually jump. "Who are you staring at?" He turns to look in the direction that I've apparently been staring in, following my gaze.

"No one," I mutter. "That guy."

"That guy standing right next to Roxy? Tommy?"

"Yeah. I like his sweater."

He looks back at Tommy, who's wearing a bright-green sweater with a fancy gay elf on it, and then over at Roxy, who's wearing a surprisingly tasteful cashmere sweater dress that hugs every one of her obnoxious, gorgeous curves, and furrows his brow at me. This guy is so fucking handsome I'd want to punch him in the face if he weren't such a good friend. "Uh-huh," he says. "Lemme help you with those bags." He takes one of the shopping bags from me.

I've got two big shopping bags filled with presents for the kids.

"Your assistant's been busy, I see."

"I'll have you know I bought these all by myself. Online. With Aimee's guidance." Now that I have one hand free, I give him a half-bro-hug. "Good to see you, man. Happy holidays."

"Welcome. Gang's all here. We'll put the presents over by the tree, okay?"

I follow him while surveying the room, in the way that I had meant to do before catching sight of Roxy fucking Carter. The gang is indeed all here, as are about thirty other people. There's a big Christmas tree in the corner of the living room that's really tastefully decorated from the middle of it up to the top and then covered with haphazard handmade decorations from about three feet down where the kids could reach the branches. When I see the hanging clay zombie with a Santa hat, I know that Finn McKay made it and smile to myself.

"The kids are all in the family room watching a movie. And destroying things, probably. What can I get you to drink? Bernie made mulled wine and eggnog, but we've got the usual full bar. Vince is making cocktails to order."

"I'll try the mulled wine."

Matt raises his eyebrows and shakes his head almost imperceptibly. A subtle warning that would cost him an arm punch if his wife caught it.

"I'll have whatever Vince wants to make me."

"Good idea."

I hear a little snort from the floor and finally notice the little Boston Terrier who's curled up in a doggy bed, anxiously looking up at me, her tail wagging. "Hey, Daisy," I say, my voice a little higher than I meant it to be. "Hey girl. I haven't seen you in a while." I bend down to pat her on her head. "She looks great! What is she now —twelve?"

"Almost thirteen," Matt says, his voice cracking a little. "She is great. Slowing down a little, but she's healthy. Lemme take your coat and grab you a drink."

I hand him my coat and then continue petting Daisy for as long as she'll let me. Being able to shower affection on a dog whenever I want to is one luxury that I do not have. A couple of years ago, after a string of bad first dates with the kind of women I had no business dating, I decided to get a dog.

That sounds weird.

I mean, I figured since Matt had basically met and

married the love of his life because she had fallen in love-at-first-sight with Daisy, maybe I'd have better luck meeting the right kind of woman if I had the right kind of dog in my life.

So, I got a dog.

I got the wrong kind of dog in my life.

I got a cute dog.

I hit the jackpot with a beautiful little cream-colored Labradoodle rescue.

I drove out to Philadelphia to get him.

I named him Jackpot.

He has his own room in my townhouse.

He has the finest dog beds in every room of my townhouse.

He has the most highly recommended dog-walker in Brooklyn.

He goes to the best dog groomer, gets the best food and chew toys.

And he fucking hates me.

He is literally the worst wingman ever.

Anytime a beautiful woman comes up to us and asks if she can pet him, he barks at her, and I'm pretty sure he's begging these women to rescue him from me, because he always tries to chase after them when they quickly walk away.

Anytime I take him to a dog park, he tries to go home with someone else.

It's humiliating.

But I love him anyway.

I'm still determined to make him love me.

A little hate never stopped me from winning anyone over eventually.

And speaking of love and hate—the little boy I love is dragging the woman who is determined to hate me over to where I'm crouched on the floor by Daisy and the Christmas tree.

"Uncle Keat!" Finn yells out as soon as he sees me. He drops Roxy's hand and runs over to tackle me, and I don't think I could love this kid any more than I do right now as I'm hugging him and grinning up at Roxy, who has her fists on her hips. She's frowning. I don't blame her—I mean, clearly, our godson prefers me over her. That's gotta hurt.

"How you doin', buddy? Long time no see."

Even though they are directly in my eyeline, I do not stare at Roxy's knee-high black boots. I also do not stare at the shapely thighs in those sheer black tights that taunt me by peeking out between the over-the-knee socks and the hem of her dress.

"Roxy's gonna show me which present is hers for me. Did you bring me a present?"

"Did I ever. I brought you three presents."

"*Seriously?*"

"Seriously." I stand up and smirk at Roxy.

"Show me!" He claps his hands together.

"Okay, but you have to wait until your parents say it's okay to open them, right?"

"Yeah, yeah."

I pull three professionally wrapped gift boxes out from one of the shopping bags for him to inspect and shake. He looks so happy. And Roxy looks so worried.

This kid is definitely coming straight to me when he runs away from home one of these days.

"Hmmm," he says. "I think I know what this one is."

"I bet you don't."

He drops the box to the floor and turns to Roxy. "Where's yours?"

That fucking Wham song, "Last Christmas" comes on, and I shudder. Tamara loved that song, and she'd play it over and over and over, from Thanksgiving to New Years. I don't think about her all that much anymore, but she sends me e-cards every Christmas, and it haunts me for weeks afterwards. Especially since the cards never say anything other than Merry Christmas. It's like she wants to make sure I don't forget her, even though she has no intention of actually keeping in touch with me or seeing me ever again.

There was a time when I would have responded to her indifference by going out and dating as many models and socialites as I could handle.

But I guess you get to a point in your life where getting the girl isn't as important to you as actually finding a girl you want to get to know and love.

Christ, that's cheesy.

But like so many of the things I rarely say out loud—it's true.

Fuck you, Wham.

Finn's exclamation of "*Yeaaahhh!*" brings me back to the room and Roxy's smug face. "I know what this is!" he shouts and jumps up and down.

"Maybe you do and maybe you don't," she says coyly.

"I know what it is, I know what it is, I know what it

is!" he chants, even as he drops it to the ground and skips off out of the room.

Roxy and I are left here to put the presents back under the tree.

"I got it," I say as she bends down next to me. Because God forbid she'd actually listen to me for once.

"You okay?" She sounds genuinely concerned, and I barely recognize her voice.

"Yeah. Why?"

"Your face just clouded over all of a sudden."

I shake my head. No need to give her a real answer. "You going somewhere later?"

"You mean like yet another holiday party? Yeah. Why?"

I shrug as we stand up. "Just wondering. You aren't exactly dressed for a family and friends Christmas party."

"Am I not?" Her fists are planted on her sexy fucking hips again. I can really only think of one time in all the years that I've known her when she hasn't assumed that stance with me. But I can't think about it right now. "And what exactly would be the appropriate attire for a single woman who's attending a family and friends Christmas party, in your opinion?" she continues. Of course she does, because she can't just drop it and not give me a hard time. "Would a bulky Rudolph sweater and corduroy pants be more to your liking?"

"Forget I said anything."

"Oh, but how could I? Every single thing you say is so perfect and memorable."

"Are you guys fighting again?" We both realize that Finn is back and he's scrunching up his little face at us.

"No!" we both say, a little too quickly and a little too loud.

"We don't fight," she says. "We just don't get along. It's fine. It doesn't affect you at all. We're still your godparents. Let's go see what the other kids are up to." She takes his hand and leads him back to the family room, and I count to myself in my head—*one, two, three*—and she gives me a saucy little glance over her shoulder before disappearing.

There it is.

That tiny opening.

Try as she might, she just can't hide that she cares, even a little bit.

A great-looking guy and the sweetest-looking lady approach me, blocking my view of the sassy loudmouth in the other room. Vince and Nina. Perfect couple number three in our circle of friends. Vince is holding out a martini glass with a candy cane hanging from the rim. He was once a bartender before becoming a minor real estate mogul, so he's always the guy to mix cocktails at parties, and every time I've let him pick something for me, he's come up with something that he knows I'll hate but will drink anyway.

"Happy holidays, big guy," he says, handing me the martini glass and slapping me on the back. "Long time no see."

"Hey there, handsome," Nina says, leaning in to kiss me.

"Hello, lovely." I'm always careful not to be too friendly with Nina, because I have no doubt that Vince would break my hand if he thought I was touching his wife inappropriately.

Christ, what's a guy gotta do to get a nice, pretty schoolteacher like this to fall for him? I look over at Vince. Be a great-looking former bad-boy with a dragon tattoo and a steady day job, I guess.

"What are you making me drink this time?" I stare down at the creamy light-pink liquid and sniff it. It is minty fresh.

"A Drunken Elf!" the asshole says, a little too eager to watch me take my first sip. "Rum and pink lemonade and candy cane. A man's drink. Bottoms up!"

I take a sip. It's actually pretty good, for a girly holiday drink that was mixed by an asshole. "It's good. Thanks."

He laughs, shaking his head. "You hate it. You don't have to drink it."

"No, I'm drinking it."

Nina rubs my arm. "So polite. Hey, are you dating anyone? If you are, you could..."

Vince shoots her a look.

"Oh, Schmidt!" She covers her mouth with both hands. So adorable. She teaches little kids, so she doesn't swear for real. "I forgot they're fully-booked. Never mind."

"Who's fully-booked?" I ask.

"Umm." She widens her eyes at Vince. "It's this..."

"It's a couples-only resort. In Antigua."

"What about it?" I ask.

"Chase hasn't mentioned it yet?" Vince looks around for Chase.

"Mentioned what?"

"It just came up all of a sudden, like—"

"Like two days ago, not even," Nina finishes his sentence, in that way that couples do.

And I can see from the look on Vince's face that he's about to rip off a bandage, in the way that only guy friends do. "We booked a week at a couples-only resort in Antigua. Around Valentine's Day."

"Oh, nice. Just the two of you?"

"Just the six of us," he says. "Chase and Aimee and Matt and Bernie too."

That sinking feeling.

I'm eight years old and finding out that I'm the only kid who didn't get invited to Jonah Kline's birthday party.

Except I'm not the only one who wasn't invited to this couples-only lovefest. I look across the room to where Roxy is standing—rather uncomfortably—talking to one of Matt's friends. Lloyd, I think his name is. I wonder if she knows about this appalling betrayal.

Vince pats me on the back. "It's nothing personal, man. It was just one of those spur-of-the-moment things that suddenly turned into a couples retreat. If you were part of a couple, you'd be coming with us."

"Sure," I say. "It's cool. I'm glad you guys are getting a vacation. I'll probably be traveling for work anyway."

"Well...as long as you aren't alone on Valentine's Day," Nina says, rubbing my arm again. Feeling sorry for me.

When did I become the guy people feel sorry for?

Because, me? I feel sorry for Lloyd. Trying to chat up

that troublemaker. She will either bite his head off or eat him alive. I think I better go save him.

"Talk to you guys later. Thanks again for the drink," I say, lifting my glass to them and strolling over to Lloyd and Roxy. I nod to Chase, who's saluting me from the family room. *Judas.*

I place the martini glass on a coaster. Fuck this drink.

"Heyyyy, Lloyd. Good to see you." I take Lloyd's hand just as he's reaching out to touch Roxy's arm, and I give it a firm shake.

"Oh hey, hi." He blinks at me, pushing his glasses up the bridge of his nose.

"Keaton. We met here last year."

"I remember, yeah. Hi."

"Hey. Happy holidays."

"Same to you."

"And to you." I wink at Roxy.

"And to you. Do you have something in your eye?"

"No, I was winking at you."

"Why?"

"Because I'm a fun, awesome guy."

"No, you aren't."

"You know Roxy? Keaton—Roxy? Roxy—Keaton?"

"We know each other fairly well," I say.

"We're friends of friends."

"Right," Lloyd says. "Course you are. I haven't seen you around at Matt and Bernie's get-togethers these past few years, though."

"Good point, Lloyd." I cross my arms in front of my chest. "Why is that, Roxy?"

She doesn't look at me. "I've been working a lot, Lloyd."

"Right, well, you were going to tell me about your job just now..."

"Was she?" I put my hand on Roxy's shoulder. "I would love to hear about your job."

"It's really not that interesting, Lloyd." She smiles at me through clenched teeth. "Why don't you tell me about *your* job, Lloyd?"

Just as Lloyd starts to tell us about his job at Matt's company, two beautiful little girls come over to grab Roxy's hands and pull her into the family room. Harriet and Joni. Harriet is Matt and Bernie's daughter, and Joni belongs to Vince and Nina.

"Hey girls," I call out.

"Hey, Uncle Keaton!" Joni yells.

"Yo, Keats!" Harriet says. Because that's how her mother addresses me.

"Excuse me, Lloyd," I walk away from him when he's in the middle of explaining something about computer engineering and follow the girls to the family room.

My so-called best friend Chase McKay is seated at a portable electric keyboard—probably the one we used to keep in the SnapLegal office, back in the day.

He's playing the intro to "Jingle Bell Rock," and Joni, Harriet, and Roxy are holding pink wireless microphones. I lean against the doorframe and watch the three of them do what may be a rehearsed routine gone awry or may just be three people moving around and bumping into each other while singing random words that are not the lyrics to this song at all.

It's cute, though.

Suddenly I feel someone rubbing my back. "Yo, Keats."

"Hey, Bernie."

"Don't call me that."

I kiss her on the cheek. "Okay. Nice party."

"Yeah. So, you heard...about the thing. Sorry. This is all Aunt Dolly's fault. And my husband's. I mean, everything's his fault, obviously. He's the worst. But also the best. It's annoying."

"It's cool. I'm glad you'll get a break. You deserve it. If you need someone to look after Daisy while you're gone, I'd be happy to do it. If I'm in town."

"Aww, that's so sweet, thanks. But Daisy and Harriet are going to be staying with my parents at the farm, so..."

"Even better." We both know that she'd never let Daisy stay with me because I must be a terrible dog daddy if my dog hates me so much. It's cool.

I'm cool.

Everything's cool.

Merry fucking Christmas to me.

CHAPTER 2
ROXY

I finally get a moment alone with Aimee in the kitchen, and I'm so happy to talk to her it's almost embarrassing.

We do a rapid-fire catch-up session, and she pours us some more white wine.

"So, work's still good?" she asks.

"Yeah, same as always. You and Chase still expanding?"

"Slowly but surely. You still dealing with that employee situation?"

"I'm dealing with it. But it's still a situation."

"How's the apartment?"

"I've been redecorating. You have to see it. It's very elegant and cozy."

"Mmm! Send me pictures! I love this dress, by the way. You look amazing. Are you seeing anyone?"

And there it is. The question I have come to dread. I take a big gulp of wine. Nobody wants to hear about how the holidays make you feel even more single than ever.

My married friends just want to hear about my sex life and how terrible the dating world is so they can simultaneously envy me for getting some *and* feel great about the fact that they don't have to deal with all the crap that goes with it anymore.

Well, I've had a great time with a lot of guys and had a lot of great sex over the years. I've had fun. A lot of fun.

But I guess you get to a certain point in your life where having fun just isn't fun anymore.

What I haven't told anyone, not even Aimee, is that almost a year ago, I made a decision. A promise to myself to stop having sex with guys who wouldn't make a good baby daddy. Not that I'm trying to get pregnant. I'm not. It's not my goal to be a single mom or anything. But I'll be turning 35 soon. If I should accidentally become pregnant—as people do—the truth is, I would probably want to have the baby. And I'd at least want the father to be involved somehow.

And it's shocking just how few of the men I had been seeing were actually men I could imagine raising a hypothetical child with. In my twenties, I found the more money a man made, the less capable he was of giving me orgasms, so most of the guys I fooled around with were really good at sex and really bad at maintaining a career or a respectable credit rating. The foxhole has basically been sealed up, so Foxy Roxy's got a whole lotta nothing to report on the man front.

"Not really," I say. "No one serious."

She groans. "I wish we knew someone we could set you up with. I keep asking Chase, but he's so protective of you. It's like no one's good enough for you."

"Well, that's sweet, I guess. And probably true." *And so hilarious that you guys don't think Keaton is good enough for me.*

Aimee polishes off her glass of wine. That was quick. "You got any vacation plans or anything coming up?"

"Nope. Do you?"

"Kind of, yeah." She goes over to the sink—to wash the wine glass or maybe just to turn her back to me. "Something just came up for February."

"Sounds like a great time to get out of New York."

"Exactly. We thought it would be a good time to go to an island. None of us has ever been on vacation without the kids, and we're planning to try again."

"Oh, you're going without the kid? Do you need me to look after him?"

She laughs. "No! I mean—thank you. But he'll stay with Chase's parents."

"Right. Wait. You're gonna have another kid?"

"Yeah. I mean, we're all planning to start trying again. Bernadette and Nina too."

"Oh. So all of your kids will be the same age. That's so cute."

"Anyway, Matt's aunt went to this couples-only resort in Antigua a few times, and she had great things to say about it. She travels a lot, you know, and she has impeccable taste. So Matt called the resort to see about reservations, and it turned out they only had three cottages available for the week around Valentine's Day. So he booked them. For the six of us. Are you mad?"

Whaaaaaat?

"I'm not mad." *I'm so freaking happy you're all going to be together, getting a tan on the dumbest day of the year, and I'll have to fend for myself in the middle of an ice storm probably.*

Her shoulders slump. "I feel guilty."

"Enough with your Midwestern guilt. I'll be fine. I'm sure there will be all kinds of parties to go to."

And that's when Nina and Bernadette walk in. It's almost as if they were waiting and listening right outside the door for Aimee to break the news to the lonely single girl about their awesome couples vacation. I still remember the days when Aimee was single and *I* was the wisecracking wise one with more experience than her, who gave her great advice and got her out of her comfort zone. Now I'm the problem child. Well, I'm one of two in this crew.

"So Keaton isn't going either?"

"No. He isn't dating anyone seriously."

"Oh."

"That we know of." She looks over at Bernadette and Nina to confirm. "Right?"

Bernadette shakes her head vehemently.

"Definitely not," Nina says.

"Good."

Aimee arches an eyebrow at me.

"I mean good, I'm glad I'm not the only mother-florking loser who isn't invited." Nina taught me how to fake-swear. It's sort of satisfying. In the way that *not* having sex with hot guys you wouldn't want to raise a kid with is satisfying.

Aimee squeezes my arm. "Honey, it's not that you

aren't invited. It's a couples-only resort and they're all booked up."

"Yeah, yeah. Sure, yeah. I didn't realize there were couples-only resorts."

"It's adults-only and couples-only. You know, it's geared toward honeymooners and people celebrating their anniversary," Bernadette says. "Boring people."

"Right. So they don't have to deal with loud children and single adults who get drunk and try to steal their spouses. That's a good angle."

"You're mad," Nina says. "I don't blame you. You know what—we should have a girls' night before we go."

"Oh my God—yes!" Aimee claps her hands, just like her son does when he gets excited. "Let's go to a movie and get drinks!"

"Or! We could kick the kids and the guys out and stay *in* to watch a movie and have drinks!" says Bernadette.

"I'm in for either option," I say. "But I gotta go. I have another party to get to. I love you guys."

Aimee pulls me in for a hug. "You're coming to our New Year's Eve thing, right?"

"Yes! Definitely. I have a few parties that night, but I'll come to yours first. Before the kids go to bed."

"Call me later," she says. "Text me when you get home."

"I'll let you know about girls' night," Nina assures me. "It's really happening this time."

"I'll walk you out." Bernadette rubs my back. "Oooh, this is so soft. I think I ordered this dress online a few months ago, but I've never worn it."

I wave to the kids and signal that I'm leaving, but I think they're so upset about my departure they're in denial. Or maybe they care more about Mario Kart. I don't know.

"How are you getting to the next place?"

"I'll just grab a cab."

"I can have my driver drop you off somewhere." I have no idea how long Keaton has been right behind us, but he is right behind us and not hiding the fact that he was staring at my ass.

"Not necessary."

"You were wearing a coat, weren't you?" Bernadette says, right before scurrying off to the bedroom.

"Yes, by all means, please just disappear and leave me alone with *this* guy!"

Keaton is grinning at me. "We aren't exactly alone. Maybe it just feels that way to you."

"Are you following me again?"

"Are you crying again?"

"Why would I cry?"

"Did you hear about the amazing couples-resort getaway that we aren't invited to?"

"Yes. Why would I cry about that? I'm not a couple. If you want to go, find a girl and book a room."

"They're fully booked for that week. I double-checked."

"Seriously? You double-checked? You actually called the couples-only resort to see if there were any rooms available?"

"I put myself on the waitlist. People cancel reservations all the time. People become one half of a couple all the time. So I hear."

"Why don't you take some girl somewhere else for Valentine's Day?"

"I just might do that."

"Fantastic. Please give the unfortunate lady my condolences."

"Well, I don't have a particular girl in mind yet, so how about I just give every lady I know and meet your condolences from now on?"

"Sounds about right."

"And you? Do you not have a particular victim in mind for a Valentine's week excursion?"

I do not have to answer that. I lower my voice. "Thanks for cockblocking me with Lloyd, by the way." I do a quick scan of the room. Lloyd is nowhere to be found. "He was nice."

"I thought so too. That's why I was pretty sure you weren't into him."

"I wasn't."

"Then you're welcome."

"I did not require your assistance. I am perfectly capable of cockblocking myself, thank you very much."

He laughs. It always surprises me when he laughs. I expect him to have an arrogant Bond villain cackle, but his eyes get all sparkly, and I hate it because it's confusing and I hate being confused. "My apologies," he says. "I suppose I underestimated your ability to repel him on your own."

Bernadette returns with my coat. "I love this coat. I think I ordered this online too. I wonder where I put it."

I hug her. "Merry Christmas," I say to her and to her only.

Keaton opens the front door for me. "Shall I call my driver?"

"Not on my account."

"Come on. I won't go with you. I'll just have him drop you off."

"Oh my darlings, look who's standing under the mistletoe!" A stylish lady in her sixties or seventies—or maybe late fifties—is standing outside the door, holding shopping bags filled with gifts. It's Matt's Aunt Dolly.

"Good evening, Dolores," Keaton says with his stupid flirty voice, stepping out onto the front steps to help her with the bags. "Happy holidays."

"Mr. Keaton Bridges, you're looking very handsome as always. Hello, Roxy, my dear gorgeous vixen."

"Lovely to see you, Dolly." I step aside. "Come on in. I was just leaving."

"I'll come in just as soon as you two beautiful young people respect the very important holiday tradition of kissing under the mistletoe."

I look up at the mistletoe that's hanging above the doorway. "Well, we aren't standing under it anymore, so..." I shrug.

"Only because I interrupted you. Go on. Don't leave an old lady hanging."

Yer killin' me, Dolores.

Keaton steps back inside and gives me a quick peck on the cheek. It's just a stupid peck on the cheek, but feeling his lips on me again gives me the stomach butterflies. I hate the stomach butterflies. I hate how good he smells. This guy has probably never held a wrench or even a screwdriver in his life. He's probably clean all the time. He probably doesn't even sweat at the gym.

"Thanks," I say. Which is dumb. It's such a dumb thing to say, but I didn't want to not say anything and appear tongue-tied just because he kissed me on the cheek. Only I can't think of any other words besides "thanks." Like I needed that or something. Like he just did me a favor.

"My pleasure," he says, grinning, and he probably does think he just did me a favor.

Asshat.

I wave Aunt Dolly inside.

Keaton gives her a quick peck on the cheek too, just to show everyone that what he did to me was no big deal.

It wasn't a big deal.

It wasn't even a small deal.

It wasn't anything.

"Have a good night, Dolores!" I sprint down the steps before she insists that the holiday tradition involves tongue.

Of course, there are no cabs around.

I text my work friend to let her know that I'm on my way to her party and walk in the direction of Fort Greene, just as I realize that it has started to snow. A tiny snowflake lands on my cheek, right where Keaton kissed me. I wipe it off because I can still feel it there. The kiss, not the snowflake.

"No luck finding a cab?"

I spin around to find Keaton a few steps behind me.

"Jesus! Don't sneak up on people like that."

"I'm pretty sure that doesn't qualify as sneaking up on you, but okay. Just let me call my driver." He's not wearing his coat, and I can see his minty-fresh breath.

"Where's your coat?"

"At their place. I'm going back."

"Well go back now. It's cold."

"Not until you get into a car."

"I will find a cab eventually. It's not that big of a deal."

"I'm calling my driver. Where are you headed?"

I sigh. "Fort Greene."

He pulls his phone out of his pocket, taps it a couple of times, and says, "Hey, can you come pick up my friend to drop her off at Fort Greene? We're on Seventh. By Barnes and Noble. Thank you." He slides the phone back into his pocket. "He'll be here in a minute."

I have to dig my nails into the palm of my balled-up hand and force myself to say: "Thank you. I appreciate it."

"No problem."

"You don't have to wait with me."

"Actually, I do. So my driver knows where to stop."

"Does your driver have a name?" I ask accusingly.

Keaton takes a deep breath before answering. "His name is Manny. He is forty-seven years old. His birthday is June tenth. He is married with three children. His wife's name is Juanita, his kids' names are Jasmine, Samuel, and Lorenzo. They live in Queens. He's a big

Yankees fan. I've employed him for seven and a half years, and he doesn't hate me at all."

"How can you tell?"

"They named their youngest son Lorenzo Keaton Perez."

I laugh. "They did not."

"You can ask him yourself."

"I plan to."

"You going to see your family? Baltimore, right?"

"Yeah, Baltimore. I'm going for a few days, that's all. You're staying here?"

"Yeah. You going to Chase and Aimee's for New Year's?"

"Yes. Are you?"

"Wouldn't miss it."

"Well, I may or may not see you there."

He crosses his fingers and holds them up. "OMG! I hope I get to see you there!"

"Are you going anywhere else that night?"

"Why?"

"Are you going to their place early, or are you going to be there for midnight, or..."

"Why don't you just tell me when you're going and ask me to show up after you've left?"

"Because that would be rude."

He shakes his head, raises his hand, and walks out to the street when a black BMW slows down. He opens the back door for me.

"Okay, thank you. I'll see you around," I say.

"Not if you can help it," he says.

As soon as I've said hello to Manny, told him where

THE PLUS ONES 41

I'm going, and fastened my seat belt, Keaton gets in beside me and shuts the car door. "Go ahead, Manny. I'll ride back with you."

I frown at him. "Really?"

"Aren't you tired of this?"

"Tired of what?"

"This dynamic."

"No. I'm fine with it."

He scrubs his face with his clean, manicured hands. "Are we cool, Roxy?"

God, it makes me nuts whenever he says my name. "Regarding?"

"You know. The wedding. What happened between us."

"What happened between us at the wedding five years ago? You're asking me now, five years later, if we're cool?"

"We haven't seen each other that many times in five years."

"Five years is five years."

He blinks. "What are you saying? Did you want me to call you the next day or something?"

I laugh. I can't help it. It's not funny. In fact, it's so not funny I sort of want to throw him in front of a bus, but I mean... He's asking me if we're cool—five years later. He's asking me if he should have called me—five years later.

He is not amused. "This is funny to you."

I can't stop laughing. I'm laughing so hard I'm crying a little.

"You think I'm an idiot for bringing it up now, but

you're the one who's been trying to avoid me all this time."

"I'm not trying to avoid you. I just don't want to see you. There's a subtle but important difference."

"You don't want to talk to me. About what happened between us."

"Nothing happened between us. We kissed."

"Uh-huh."

"I mean, it was a good kiss. Good kisses happen. To people. All the time."

"Uh-huh."

"What is there to talk about?"

"Can you just answer this one question, and then I will never bring up this subject again, I promise you."

"What?"

"Are you actually mad at me for not calling you after we kissed? Were you mad at me? Be honest."

Am I? Was I? Sort of? Maybe? I can't answer this question.

"Oh my God," he says, slapping his hand to his forehead. "All this time you've been thinking I'm an asshole for not calling you."

"I think you're an asshole for all kinds of reasons."

"Have you ever been in a serious relationship in your life?"

"Why would you ask that?"

"Because you act like someone who has never been in a serious relationship in her life."

"How would you even know how I act? We don't really know each other. Just because we have the same best friends—"

"Why is it so important to you to believe that?"

"It's not important to me. It's true!"

"Is it? Is that what's true? That you and I don't have any kind of connection? Because we're different? Because I was a dick to my best friend and yours over seven years ago for like a month? Because another thing that's true is that Chase and Aimee and I all made peace with each other and I became best friends with Aimee too and our circle of friends grew and included each other. And then everyone else got married and had kids except us, and one summer night on the deck of a loft in Greenpoint at our best friends' wedding, you and I felt something—it may not have been for each other, but we felt something together—and we kissed. And it was a great fucking kiss and I liked it, and that doesn't mean it had to mean anything more than that. But it happened and it happened between us. And you walked away from me because you didn't want it to become anything else, and that's fine. But it's not fine for you to be mad at me because you think I should have called you, even though you made it very clear to me that you didn't want it to go anywhere. You can be mad at me if you want, but you do not get to be mad at me for that."

My eyes are stinging. I have no idea what just happened. One minute we're chatting on a sidewalk, and the next he's mad at me. He doesn't get to be mad at me!

Why do I feel so much closer to him right now?

Why am I so turned-on right now?

I slide as far away from him as I can, backed up into the corner of the back seat, right up against the door.

His eyebrows shoot up. "Are you afraid I'm going to hit you?"

No, idiot, I'm afraid I'm going to straddle you and never stop kissing you.

"I think I should get out here."

"No." He waves off that idea. "If you really can't handle talking about it—I'm done talking. I'll go to Chase and Aimee's at ten thirty on New Year's Eve. How's that? Does that work for you? Because I will be going to Chase and Aimee's. I will be going to hang out with my best friends, whether you're there or not. Whether you like it or not."

This is the most intense and weird conversation I've had with anyone in years, including the time a crazy homeless woman cornered me on the F train and told me we knew each other in a past life.

This is the most I've *felt* all year.

It can't be Keaton Bridges who made me feel this much.

This is humiliating.

Manny slows down and pulls over in front of my friend's row house.

I have to say something before I get out.

Anything.

I clear my throat. "Thank you, Manny."

"Have a good night, miss."

I don't look at Keaton, but I turn my head slightly in his direction. "Thanks for the ride. I'll, uh...I'll be at Chase and Aimee's at eight. Merry Christmas. Happy New Year if I don't see you."

"Same to you," he says.

I nod. "Good night." I get out of the car and shut the door, taking care not to slam it.

The car drives off before I step to the curb.

What. Just. Happened?

My hands are trembling when I pull my phone out of my pocket. I have his number. I've never called or texted him directly, but we do group texts all the time.

I have no idea what I should say to him in a text, but I can't just leave things like this.

Can I?

Maybe I should.

We're both just in a bad mood because of the holidays.

We're both just annoyed because we don't have a real boyfriend or girlfriend to get into a fight with.

It'll blow over.

Or maybe I'll finally convince Chase and Aimee to have two separate birthday parties for Finn every year. We can do a time-share the next time Aimee gives birth. I'll definitely leave the New Year's Eve party by nine thirty.

I slip my phone back into my pocket.

We can definitely avoid each other, for the most part, for at least another five years or so.

It'll be fine.

CHAPTER 3
KEATON

* Early February *

"Just go. Come on. I'm begging you. I appreciate that you have your principles and you know what you want and what you don't want. But there is no ideal situation that I can create for you right now that will make you happy. However, I know for a fact that both of us will feel better about literally everything if you just go."

All of New York is covered in gray snow and slush, and my dog refuses to take a dump outside unless the ground is solid, perfectly level, and above sixty-five degrees Fahrenheit. All winter I've kept the floors in his room covered with pee pads. All winter he's been relieving himself on the floors of my two-million-dollar townhouse and then getting cabin fever because he refuses to go for walks with me. I put waterproof dog boots on him. He's wearing a doggy coat. I've tried to coax him with treats. I've got my biodegradable poop bag ready to go. All around us, dogs are defecating and their owners are getting on with their Sunday, but my dog—my adorable furry demon child—is refusing to squat, move, or acknowledge my existence.

I am internationally renowned for being a skilled negotiator when it comes to business deals of all kinds. I once literally charmed the socks off my opponent in a tennis match back in high school. There is only one woman on earth I haven't been able to convince to go out with me, and she is now the mother of my best friend's child, so I'm fine with that. But there is literally nothing I can say or do to convince this canine to shit in the snow.

I am so fucking ready for this winter to be over. The only trips I've taken in the past couple of months have been to Chicago, Seattle, and Toronto. I haven't seen the sun in weeks. I can't even remember the last time I socialized with anyone unless it was a dinner meeting. The gang cancelled our monthly brunch because they all have so much to do before going on their little couples getaway next week, so after I get home and dry Jackpot off—if he'll let me—I plan to look into a last-minute weekend getaway to some tropical island. By myself. Because why the fuck not. There's no shame in it. Maybe I'll go to one of those resorts for singles only. They still have those, right?

"Right, buddy?" I say to the dog who's supposed to be my buddy. He looks straight ahead at nothing in particular. I feel my phone vibrate in my pocket, pull it out, and see that it's Vince Devlin calling. Probably to ask me to do him some kind of favor so he can get out of town next week with his wife. Not like I've got anything better to do.

"Mr. Devlin."

"Hey man, you got a minute?"

I look down at Jackpot, who is standing perfectly still, like no dog ever. "Yeah. What's up?"

"Just wondering what you got planned for next week and if you can take a few days off from work."

"Why?"

"Turns out Nina and I won't be able to go to that resort in Antigua...What?...I'm talking to him now...Nina says 'hey.'"

"Hey, Nina."

"Are you flirting with my wife?"

"Nope. You were saying?"

"Nina's parents were gonna fly in to stay with Joni because my dad and stepmom are on a cruise and my brother's looking after Charlie and they both have the flu. Anyway, her dad just threw his back out. He can't move, so Nina's mom has to stay with him. Now we're all just gonna go to Indiana to be with my in-laws for a week."

"Yeesh."

"Yeah. I mean, they're nice. It's fine. So do you want our reservation? You got some girl you can take?"

I am shocked—*shocked*—by the first girl who comes to mind when he asks me this. "Yeah. Definitely."

"Yeah?"

"Definitely. Send me the info, I'll Venmo the money."

"No rush."

"I will Venmo the money immediately."

"Okay, cool. Glad this worked out for you."

"I mean, I'm not glad your father-in-law threw his back out, but thanks for calling me."

"Course. Who's the girl?"

"I'll let you know." I end the call and consider my options.

I perused the resort's website last month out of curiosity. They are strictly a couples-only establishment, but it's not like you have to be married. They just don't cater to single guests. I could easily convince one of the women I've dated over the past few years to accompany me. What am I saying? I wouldn't *have* to convince any of them. All I'd have to do is ask. Problem is—I wasn't even interested in asking any of them out for a second date. Do I really want to deal with introducing one of them to my best friends and hope that they all get along?

Or...

Do I want to try to convince the one woman who I know gets along with my best friends that it wouldn't be the worst thing in the world to have to share a cottage with me in paradise and pretend to like me in front of the hotel staff for one week?

I finally lead Jackpot back toward home, and just as I'm about to call Chase to ask him how he thinks I should handle this, Aimee comes up on my Caller ID. I pull my dog under the Rite Aid awning before answering.

"Mrs. McKay."

"Hi! Hey—I just called Roxy to ask if she had a guy

she wanted to take to the resort, and then Vince texted to say that you're paying for his reservation. Who are you taking?"

That sinking feeling again.

"Who did Roxy say she wanted to take?"

"Nobody. She said to ask you."

I cannot control the stupid smile that's spreading across my face. "She said she wants to go with me?"

She laughs at that. Hard. "Um, no. She said to ask you if you want to go with someone else. She doesn't want to go at all."

"Why doesn't she want to go? Is she crazy...*er* than we thought she was?"

"I don't know. She didn't really want to talk about it."

Of course she didn't.

"But I mean...if you don't mind staying in a cottage with her for a week...I would really love to hang out with her there. Both of you, I mean. I think she really does want to go, and I mean, if there's a zombie apocalypse in Brooklyn while we're gone and there's no one here to help Roxy out, I would never forgive myself."

"I'm pretty sure the zombies will leave her alone as soon as she opens her mouth."

She snort-laughs at that. Long and hard. "That's not funny. Look, I know how you guys feel about each other, but I think I speak for all of us when I say that we miss both of you and it would be great to spend some time with you for real."

How do Roxy and I feel about each other, exactly? Please tell me. "Does she still live where you used to live?"

"Yes. You aren't going to go over there, are you?"

"I do not expect her to respond to my texts or calls."

"Why not?"

"Because of how we feel about each other."

"Right. Well. Text her first. She hates it when people just show up uninvited."

"I would like to remind you that I am a properly socialized human being."

"I would like to remind you that Roxy isn't. She will knee you in the balls. She once made a guy cry when he showed up at our dorm with flowers and chocolates when she was trying to study for an exam. But she's got a good heart."

"And I've got balls of steel. I can handle her."

She snort-laughs again. "Sure you can. Wait—Finn! Put that back in the garbage! I gotta go."

And that was the longest phone conversation I've had with her in almost five years.

Jackpot barks at me. "Just give me a minute. Look—there's hardly any snow on the sidewalk here!" I tell him. "Do your thing." He stares at me blankly and then looks away.

I am three blocks from my place and six blocks from Roxy's. As much as I want to take the dog home—a guy should only have to deal with one asshole at a time—I still need to establish myself as the alpha in this relationship. Fuck, I still need to establish this as a relationship. Between Jackpot and me, I mean.

And between Roxy and me, let's be real.

I've never texted her directly before, just group texts. But here goes.

ME: This is Keaton Bridges. I'm taking you to Antigua next week. You at home right now?

I do not expect any kind of response, but the moving dots appear immediately.

ROXY CARTER: You are not, and none of your business.

ME: We'll be there in ten minutes.

ROXY CARTER: Who's we?

ME: You'll see.

ROXY CARTER: Do not come over.

ME: So you are at home.

ROXY CARTER: None of your business, and I am not going to Antigua with you.

I put the phone in my pocket and tug on Jackpot's leash. "Let's go, boy," I say in my deepest, most authoritative voice. It works. He immediately follows, and I try not to show how surprised and grateful I am. I make a mental note to use the same tone with Roxy.

About ten minutes later, we're in front of her building on Clinton. The last time I was standing here, I got shot down by her former roommate, but I am in no mood to take "no" for an answer today. I buzz "R. Carter" and fully expect to have to call her, but I'm greeted with static and a husky voice.

"What?"

"That how you always answer your intercom?"

"Yes."

"Figures. Come down and talk to me for a minute."

"No thanks."

THE PLUS ONES 53

"Come on. I've got my dog with me. I don't want him getting your apartment dirty."

"Neither do I." There's a short pause. "You have a dog?"

"You know that."

"I had no idea you had a dog. Why would I know that?"

"Will you please just come down? Unless you want to let us up. These are your options."

"Or I could just not come down or let you up."

"I will wait here until someone lets me in."

"This building has a *no dog* policy."

"Well, I have a *quit fucking around and get down here now* policy."

"I'm not going to Antigua with you."

"Come down and let me calmly explain to you why you are."

I get no response. No static. No buzz, no door clicking open.

She's coming down. I know she is. She knows I'll just keep bugging her if she doesn't.

"She's coming down," I say to Jackpot. "Look cute." He's facing away from me, staring up the street. "Good boy."

A minute later, a blonde in a long puffy black coat and winter boots comes to the door, and somehow, I forget to breathe.

Those ice blue eyes are fixed on mine in something between a glare and a dare, and I cannot look away.

I take a step back when she opens the door. Fucking hell, she looks good. Even in a puffy coat and winter boots. I haven't seen her since the Christmas party and that weird argument or whatever it was in my car afterwards. "Your hair's different" is what I say before I can think of something a little less lame.

She brushes a few loose strands out of her face and says, "Yeah. This is your dog?"

"Yeah."

"Are you sure?"

"Would you like to see the adoption papers?"

"I think he's the one who needs to see them. What's his name?"

"Jackpot."

"Hey, Jackpot." She bends down, and all of a sudden, Jackpot's tail is wagging and he turns around to jump up on her legs. "Hey, boy. You're so cute. Look how cute you are! Look at you in your little coat and your little boots. We match! We match, don't we?" Jackpot barks once in agreement, and then Roxy stands up and gets in my face. "I don't want to go with you."

"But you want to go to the resort, I mean—have you seen how gorgeous it is?"

"Aimee sent me a link to the website. Of course it's gorgeous. I'm sure I'll go there someday."

"You want to go with Chase and Aimee and Matt and Bernadette."

"Yes, I do. I just don't want to go with you."

"We'll both be asleep for most of the time we're alone together."

"I doubt that. They're all going to want to spend time alone together as couples. That's kind of the point."

"Not only. If that were the point, they would have all taken separate vacations."

She purses her lips and looks down at Jackpot, who's still staring up at her and wagging his tail. She's got nothing to say to that because she knows I'm right.

"Aimee really wants you to go. I'm sure Bernie does too."

She looks off into the distance, at nothing in particular, just not at me.

"I'm paying Vince for the cottage, and I will cover all of your travel expenses."

"I have money. I don't need you to pay for my plane ticket."

"I know you don't *need* me to pay for your plane ticket, Roxy. I'm offering to buy your plane ticket. There are no strings attached to the offer. I won't expect anything from you, other than your usual charming and delightful company. No one will think any less of you because you accepted a man's offer to pay for your travel expenses."

She fans her face. "Oh my God, I think I just swooned."

"Just go. Come on. I'm begging you. I appreciate that you have your principles and you know what you want and what you don't want. But there is no ideal situation that I can create for you right now that will make you happy. However, I know for a fact that both of us will feel better about literally everything if you just go."

She blinks twice, and those words have the exact same effect on her as they did on Jackpot. "Isn't there some other girl you can pay to pretend to be your girl-friend or something?"

"Honestly, I don't think it would be right to go with anyone other than you. None of us like the idea of you being here alone while we're all out of town."

She scoffs at that. "I won't be alone."

I sigh. *Here it is:* "Consider this my way of making amends. I don't like the idea of you being mad at me for not calling you after Chase and Aimee's wedding."

She narrows her eyes at me, and her fists go straight to those hips that are really fucking sexy, even though they're completely hidden by a padded winter coat. "I thought I wasn't allowed to be mad at you for that."

"To be clear, this does not mean that I believe you have a valid reason for being mad at me for this long. But whatever else I may be, I am a gentleman, and a gentleman always calls after...that kind of thing. No matter what. It was wrong of me not to. And I am apologizing for that now."

I can see the tension melting from her face and body.

"Even though you've been an irrational stubborn asshole about it for over five years."

She rolls her eyes. "Dude. Know when to stop talking."

"I'm done."

She stares down at Jackpot again. "Why does he look so uptight?"

"He hasn't taken a shit yet today."

"Why not?"

"He doesn't like to go on the snow. I can't make him."

She screws up her face at me, takes a step closer to

Jackpot, uses her foot to clear snow away from a large patch of cement next to him, points to it, and says, "Jackpot. Do your business. Right now. Right there."

My dog makes a weird grumbly noise, steps over to the cleared patch, turns around a few times, squats, and lays a miracle turd while looking up at her.

"Atta boy! Good boy!" she says.

I would say the same, but I'm too stunned to speak. I pull the small bag from my pocket and pick up my dog's perfectly formed poop with it.

"Atta boy," she says to me.

I hand her the leash and walk over to the nearest trash bin. That did not make her the alpha in this relationship, but it did impress the shit out of both me and Jackpot. I guess I'm an idiot and an asshole for not thinking to clear away snow for my dog. Whatever. I would have figured it out eventually.

When I return to Roxy, all I can say is: "You need to come with me."

"Yeah. Fine. I'll go. But I'm not 'going with you.' I'm going to be with Aimee and Chase and Matt and Bernadette. I'm going to get out of this wintry cesspool of a city, and I'm going to get a tan. I'm going to that resort *despite* the fact that I will have to share a cottage with you."

"And a plane ride."

"We don't have to fly together."

"We do have to give the impression of being a couple in public."

"Whatever. Just send me the information. I'm not sharing a bed with you."

"Fair enough."

"I'm not kissing you."

"Famous last words."

"I mean it."

"Fair enough."

She looks down at Jackpot, who hasn't stopped staring up at her like he's madly in love. "Who's gonna look after this guy?"

"He stays at a really great dog hotel when I'm out of town. No kennels. He likes it there."

"I bet. I'm sure he's thrilled to get a break from you."

I hold out my hand for her to give the leash back to me. She places the handle in my palm and crouches down to rub my dog's head. "It was nice meeting you, Mr. Jackpot."

He barks at her. A not at all subtle plea for her to take him with her.

"Sorry, buddy," she says as if she understood him. "I'm not allowed to have dogs in my building, so I'm afraid you're stuck with this guy."

"I'm a good dog dad," I say a little too defensively. "He just doesn't like me yet."

She stands up again. "How long have you had him?"

"Couple of years. We gotta go. I'll be in touch. What color's your bikini? We should coordinate."

She flips me the bird as she heads back inside.

"Right. Surprise me. I'll bring shorts in all the colors." I tug on Jackpot's leash and start to walk away before I get too caught up thinking about what that woman looks like in a bikini. "Come on, boy."

"Go home, Jackpot!" Roxy orders, staring at my dog and pointing at me.

Jackpot whines, but he obeys her. I don't look back because I don't need to see the smug look on her pretty face. I expect to get an eyeful of that look and everything else for one week straight.

I also don't look back because I can't stop smiling and she does not need to know that.

CHAPTER 4
KEATON

Today's the day.

I feel like I'm getting ready to go to summer camp to see my friends, except instead of sharing a cabin in the woods with a bunch of farting adolescent boys, I'll be in a cottage on an island in the West Indies with a blazing hot woman who despises me. And instead of saying good-bye to my parents (one of whom might actually miss me), I'm saying good-bye to a dog whom I know for a fact will not miss me.

I know this because I'm trying to say a heartfelt good-bye to him before going to the office for a meeting, but he's way too busy saying "hi" to the owners of the dog hotel to notice.

"Okay, bye, buddy." I rub his back, and he barks happily at the nice lady who's now holding his leash. I tell her I'll check in with them tonight, I ask her to send pics and videos, I say good-bye to Jackpot one more time just in case he didn't hear me the first couple of times, and then leave before I really embarrass myself.

Manny is double-parked outside, and just as I'm getting into the car, I get a call from Chase.

"Hey. Shouldn't you be on a plane right now?"

"We'll be boarding soon. Just calling to remind you that if you fuck around with my wife's best friend, I will castrate you."

"That is so sweet of you to remind me. Define fucking around." I signal to Manny that he can drive.

"Any kind of penetration of any part of her body with any of your body parts. Including the metaphorical penetration of her heart."

"I can't help it if people fall madly in love with me when I'm not even trying to be charming. Define castration."

"The slow and painful removal of your testicles."

"You're so literal. Does Aimee know you're making this call?"

"I mean it. I've seen the way you check her out."

"How does Aimee feel about it? Because I bet she'd be thrilled if we got together."

"In what world are you and Roxy going to get together? I'm saying don't hook up with her, don't be a dick to her, don't be too nice to her, don't forget that you're just pretending to be her boyfriend for the sake of the hotel staff and the other guests, and you are in no way obligated or allowed to pretend to be her anything when you're in the room alone together."

"I'm not 'allowed?' Put Aimee on."

"Trust me, if you fuck with Roxy, you will be begging me to protect you from Aimee."

"Did it ever occur to you that Roxy might *want* me to

penetrate one or more of her parts?"

He's quiet for a moment, and I know he's squeezing his phone, and I think I can hear the steam shooting out of his ears.

"I'm just messing with you, asshole. I have no intention of fucking with Roxy. We're oil and water." As soon as I say the words "oil and water," I picture myself in the shower with a tanned, naked, oiled-up Roxy Carter—but that doesn't mean I'm going to fuck with her. That means I'm a straight human male. "So don't even worry about it. We're both just going because we want to hang out with you guys. Although right now I'm trying to remember why I've missed hanging out with you so much."

"Yeah, it'll be fun. I'm glad you're going. I just had to say it so we're clear. We'll see you there. Safe flight."

"You too. See you there."

Chase "Straight No Chaser" McKay. That guy. We used to work together. Well, I guess, technically I worked for him when I was the CFO at his legal tech startup, but I was his first investor and I was on the board, so we were pretty equally weighted in terms of power as far as I was concerned. We have long since sold SnapLegal for ten times my initial investment, and he started a thriving business with his wife and I became a full-time venture capitalist. So he's not the boss of me. At all. But I've always liked that he'd give it to me straight, ever since college. It's why he's my best friend. I just like it less when we're discussing my personal life, and I like it very little right now. But he's not wrong. And I have no intention of fucking with Roxy.

I don't even have to wonder if anyone's giving her the

same warning.

They aren't.

By the time I get to my office and my assistant has handed me the notes for my meeting, I pull out my personal phone and see a few messages on the lock screen from my Friends group. They're probably all at the airport now, except for Roxy and me. Vince, Nina, and Joni are going to Indiana. Aimee, Chase, Bernie, and Matt are all flying out to Antigua together. I couldn't get Roxy and me onto the same flight as our friends because I couldn't justify rescheduling my morning meeting. Yet another reason for Roxy to be mad at me.

AIMEE MCKAY: I would just like to officially announce in text form how happy I am that Roxy and Keaton are finally a couple! <heart eyes emoji>
BERNIE FARMER: #ROXTON4EVA
ROXY CARTER: <raised middle finger emoji>
NINA DEVLIN: Roxy and Keaton sittin' in a palm tree...
VINCE DEVLIN: F-A-K-I-I-N-G. Yes I know I spelled it wrong.
CHASE MCKAY: Congrats and keep your hands to yourself, KB
ME: What, these hands? <two raised middle

finger emojis>

AIMEE MCKAY: Awww, their emojis match!

BERNIE FARMER: Do you have any thoughts on the matter that you'd like to share with the group, dear husband?

MATT MCGOVERN: I'm literally sitting right next to you, darling wife. Why don't you just ask me with your sweet voice?

BERNIE FARMER: Because you're staring at your phone. This is how Matt feels about it, you guys: <neutral face emoji>

MATT MCGOVERN: I am in fact delighted by and for the adorable fake couple.

ROXY CARTER: I hate all of you.

ME: Oh honey, you don't mean that.

ROXY CARTER: Especially you, Bridges.

AIMEE MCKAY: So cute. We have to board now guys. See you there!!!!!

I cannot fucking wait to get some quality time with those people.

Now I just have to get Oiled-up Shower Roxy out of my head before I go into my meeting and before I pick her up in a couple of hours.

I have not been able to get Oiled-up Shower Roxy out of my head for the past two hours. I don't even know what I said in that meeting, and I've already forgotten who I was meeting with. My brain is a dick. All of a sudden, I'm glad it's so cold in New York, because Roxy emerges from her building all covered-up with winter clothes. Layers of clothes. So many layers of clothes between me and her naked, probably not oiled-up or wet body.

I step out of the back seat of the car, and I'm greeted with a classic frown.

"Good day," I say.

"Good day," she mutters.

When Manny comes around to take her luggage, she presents him with all of the warmth and smiles that she's withholding from me.

"You got your passport?" I ask.

She rolls her eyes.

"It's a valid question."

"An eye roll is a valid answer. Do *you* have your passport?"

I smile. "Yes, I do. Thank you so much for asking." I gesture for her to get into the back seat. She smells like cocoa butter. I wonder if she's already wearing suntan lotion. I wonder if she's wearing a bikini under there. Maybe she's planning on stripping down to her bikini as soon as we land in Antigua. That seems like the kind of thing Roxy would do.

I am so fucked.

I get into the car and keep my eyes straight ahead for a good five minutes, I'd say. At first Roxy is typing on her phone, and then I can see out of the corner of my eye that she's watching me not look at her. She is amused. She is such a jerk.

"How's it going over there?"

"Fine. Have you been to Antigua before?"

"No. Have you?"

"No. But I've been to St. Barts, the Caymans, Turks and Caicos."

"Of course you have."

"And you? Have you been to any of the Caribbean islands before?"

"I have not yet had the pleasure, no."

"Really?"

"Why is that so surprising?"

"They're so close to the East Coast."

She shrugs. "I like Florida."

I roll my eyes and say nothing.

She snorts. "Do we not approve of the Sunshine State? I thought rich white people liked the art scene and the party scene down there."

"I've never been all that into art or partying." I glance down at the leather messenger bag by her feet and see that she's brought her laptop. "You planning to do some work while you're there?"

"A little. Aren't you?"

"A little."

I look out the window and continue to think about Oiled-up Shower Roxy because I have completely lost control of my fucking brain and she just smells like she wants to be naked. That cocoa butter is sexually assaulting my olfactory system. I can feel her watching me and smirking. I am quite certain that she knows I'm having sex thoughts and that it amuses her. She is the worst fake girlfriend ever, and I just want to stick my head under her shirt for five minutes and then I'm done. It's out of my system.

She's not even my type.

I mean—Roxy Carter is every man's type.

But she's not *my* type.

She's made it perfectly clear that I'm not her type.

Everyone we know has made it clear that I'm not her type.

I am well aware of the fact that I still have a tendency to long for the women I know I can't have.

So I won't dwell on her.

This trip isn't about her.

It's definitely not about showering with her.

"Wow, you are an even more fun travel companion than I expected you to be."

I do not look over at her when I say, "I thought you would appreciate it if I gave you some space."

"I do, thanks! And I'd really appreciate it if you'd figure out a way to be a little less obvious when you're having pervy thoughts about me, because it's creeping me out."

I slowly turn to glare at her. "Trust me, it's unpleasant for me too."

"I'm not having sex with you."

"I'm aware of that."

"So pull it together and think about something else."

"You know what, just keep talking. Every word you utter is like a bucket of cold water being tossed on my pants."

"Did you just say the word 'utter' out loud? You are so pretentious. I do not utter words."

"You're right. I meant 'spew.'"

"You know what—let's go back to not talking."

"Fantastic idea."

"I'm sure I've sufficiently uttered enough boner-reducing words already."

"I did not have a boner—I'm not eleven—and yes, you have."

She yanks her scarf off her neck, angrily unzips her coat, and takes it off in a way that is both violent and somehow really fucking sexy and also evil because now I have to look at her in a really thin cardigan over a tight black top.

Hello!

Perhaps someone should not have removed her coat if she didn't want to reveal just how aroused she is right now.

"Warm in here," she says.

Really? Because you look a little cold to me, Roxy Carter.

"How long until we get to the airport?"

"About another half hour, miss," Manny says.

She exhales loudly and peels off her cardigan, exposing a tight black tank top and her toned bare arms. She lifts her hair up off her neck, revealing the tie straps of a bright red bikini under her tank top. She glances over at me, smirks for like one second, and then lets her hair fall back down around her neck and turns to look out her window.

She's the fucking devil.

And I want to stick my head under that tank top for twenty minutes and then I'm done.

CHAPTER 5
ROXY

'm the devil, I know.

But he needed to know who he's dealing with.

If you've got a penis, do not try to convince Foxy Roxy that you aren't having a party in your pants, because I don't even have to look at your pants to know what's going on down there. I know semi-face when I see it. Keaton Bridges has had it ever since his car showed up at my place.

I must say, though, he looks very attractive with his jaw clenched. And he really has been very polite and restrained so far. Now that we're at the airport, I have removed my down jacket again, and he helped me to roll it up and shove it into the little pouch it came with so I could pack it into my suitcase. I thanked him by not commenting on how weird it was that he was inhaling so deeply while in my personal space.

We're heading for the VIP lounge, and he's had this goofy lopsided grin on his face ever since we checked in. That stupid dimple.

"What?"

"Your name is Roxanne? Roxanne Carter? I saw it on your luggage tag."

"Is that amusing to you? Roxy is short for Roxanne."

"I didn't realize. I've only ever heard you called Roxy."

"You thought my parents took one look at me when I was born and said, 'This baby looks like a porn star. Let's call her Roxy!'"

"So you gave yourself a porn star name?"

"People started calling me Foxy Roxy in college. I mean, half the people did. The other half called me Franzia."

He wrinkles his nose. "Why?"

"Because I'm classy as a box of fridge wine."

He shakes his head. "I don't see that. I don't like that for you. Did Aimee call you that?"

"No. She's the one who started calling me Foxy Roxy."

"Good. You're definitely not a Franzia." He seems genuinely upset by this. It's kinda cute.

"You got a better nickname for me?"

"Not yet. I will."

Before I have the chance to assure him that he can't possibly know me well enough to give me a nickname, a middle-aged man calls out Keaton's name as he passes by in the concourse. Keaton does a double-take and stops to talk to him, so I wait a few feet away.

"Tom? Hey."

"Hey, good to see you!"

Keaton extends his hand to shake Tom's, but Tom gives him a one-armed hug.

"Good to see you, Keaton. Wow, long time."

"Yeah, yeah yeah. Hi."

"Where you headed?"

"I'm just meeting up with some friends in Antigua for a few days. You?"

"Niiiice. I'm just back from Miami. Conference."

"Great. Sounds fun."

"Oh boy. A little too much fun, if you must know."

Keaton emits the fakest and most awkward laugh I hope to ever hear, and after these two men stare at each other while smiling for another ten awful seconds, Tom finally looks over at me and says, "Hi. I'm Tom."

I wave at him. "Roxanne. Hello."

"Oh sorry, yeah, that's my friend Roxy. We're just heading to the—"

"Yeah yeah yeah, I won't keep you. So maybe I'll see you around, now that Tam's gonna be back in town..."

Keaton looks like he just got slapped in the face. "She is?"

"Oh, you haven't heard? Tamara's moving back to New York. Next month...by herself. She's crazy busy. You know how she gets. I'm sure she's planning to get in touch."

"Sure, yeah. Well, she didn't mention it. At all. But that's great. Good for her. Great to see you, Tom. We gotta..."

Tom nods and waves and walks off.

Keaton stares at the floor as we continue on our way.

So, his ex-girlfriend is moving back to New York and she didn't tell him. That's gotta hurt. I guess. "You okay?"

"Yup."

And that's all he says for the next twenty minutes.

We get coffee and snacks in the fucking amazing lounge that I have never been in before, and he just angrily types emails on his laptop.

A message from Aimee comes in on our group text, and we both open it at the same time. It's a shot of the view from their cottage veranda at the resort. It's fucking amazing. The tops of palm trees and every shade of blue and green, from the sea to the islands across the bay to the sky, and huge fluffy white clouds that you want to reach out and touch.

AIMEE MCKAY: You guys. You. Will. Not. Believe. You will not even believe!

BERNADETTE FARMER: I am never leaving this place. I feel like Harriet and Daisy will be very happy on the farm with my parents. Or with Matt if he doesn't want to stay with me.

MATT MCGOVERN: I'll miss them a lot, but I'm not leaving.

Chase sends another picture, this one's of their private infinity plunge pool.

ME: OMG I cannot get there fast enough. So excited to see all of you! Except Keaton.

I look over at Keaton. Nothing. He's staring at the picture, and he is as expressionless as Matt McGovern.

VINCE DEVLIN: Gorgeous! Happy for you guys. Also, maybe start another group text for when you're at the resort that doesn't include me and Nina? If I see one more picture of that place I will jump out a window.
VINCE DEVLIN: FYI, that is not a dark joke because the tallest building in Indiana is like four floors.
NINA DEVLIN: Not funny, hon. But yeah, maybe start another group chat for the week. <sad face emoji> Have fun!

Keaton shuts his laptop without responding to the texts.

"Are you sure you're okay?"

"Yup." He stands up. "I'm getting a gin and tonic. You want anything?"

I try to suppress any kind of facial or vocal expression that would betray that I'm inwardly making fun of his unbelievable WASP-ishness. "I'll have a beer, thanks. Any kind."

He nods and walks off, and I can't help noting how good he looks in jeans. This guy should wear jeans more often. He needs to loosen up. A lot. He seemed happy when he was with Tamara. Maybe when she's back she can loosen him up. Who knows.

He returns with a bottle of Blue Moon, which is a coincidence because it's my favorite beer. "I told him you don't need a glass. Was I correct in doing so?"

"You were indeed." I take the bottle from him, and he clinks his glass against it before taking three big gulps of his G&T. "I love Blue Moon."

"I know." He doesn't even sit down. He finishes his highball of gin and tonic and returns to the bar for a refill.

This should be interesting.

When he reclaims his seat next to me, he has already polished off nearly half of his second cocktail and his entire being has loosened up significantly.

"Feelin' better?" I ask.

"Feelin' fine," he says. "I can't fucking wait to get there. You excited?"

"Yes. Thank you for convincing me to come."

He cocks his head, looking a little more surprised than I'd like. Is it really that shocking to hear me say "thank you"?

"You're welcome." His eyes drop to my rack for a brief second. "I just hope you can handle seeing me shirtless." His voice has changed. It's that golden voice that Aimee told me about years ago, when they first met and he was hitting on her. It's a good voice, I'll give him that.

"Oh yeah? Most women can't handle it, I assume?"

"Most women lose their minds. But you'll have to control yourself." He leans in and whispers, "You'll have to constantly remind yourself that I'm only pretending to be your boyfriend."

"Trust me, it's all I'll be thinking about."

"Trust me, you'll be thinking about how good I look in shorts. And FYI, I did just happen to bring a red pair, so we *will* match."

Normally, I would be verbally slaughtering him for

his stupid tipsy horny bravado, but for now, I will take flirtatious Keaton over silent, unhappy Keaton.

For now.

"I hope you also brought a pair of tasteful leopard print, black, and also white shorts so we match every day."

"You only brought four swimsuit options? What about Day Five and Six?"

I lean in and whisper, "I plan to spend two days sunbathing completely naked."

I watch his Adam's apple bob up and down. He tilts his head toward me so that his lips are dangerously close to mine. "I plan to spend *five* days sunbathing completely naked. So we'll match three days out of six."

CHAPTER 6
KEATON

"Okay, *now* I have a boner," I mutter, loud enough that only my mildly inebriated fake girlfriend can hear.

She giggles. This is like the fifth time I've made her giggle today, and I'm secretly over the moon. Her usual laugh is this controlled husky chuckle that always seemed manufactured to me. I had suspected her real laugh was some evil witch cackle, but she makes this musical girly sound that's completely charming and nothing like the rest of her.

But neither that, nor the prospect of seeing this woman in a bikini is the most boner-inducing thing in my life at the moment.

It's the tropical wet dream we're going to be living in for the next six nights.

Now that we've stepped out of the slightly rickety ancient shuttle that brought us here from the airport, I can safely say that Roxy Carter is not the most jaw-droppingly beautiful and sexy thing I can see for miles.

Okay, she's not the *only* jaw-droppingly beautiful and sexy thing I can see for miles.

The Coco Beach Resort is a knockout. I want to drop to my knees in gratitude. I mean, I like New York, and I don't know if I could ever really live anywhere else long-term—but this is heaven on earth and I already feel better than I've felt in years.

I can't decide what to stare at—the vibrant lush flora, the carpet of mowed lawn at our feet, the expanse of blue sky and friendly white clouds overhead, the brightly painted cottages all around the cliffside of the peninsula, the peek-a-boo view of the white sand beach and crystal clear sea that lie just beyond the infinity pool, or the impossibly erect nipples that have been protruding through the fabric of Roxy's top since she removed her coat back in New York.

It is most definitely not cold here in Antigua, Roxy Carter.

I tip Ajay the driver before he grabs our suitcases and carries them down the paved path to the cottage with the front desk and lobby.

"I'll let them know we're here," Roxy says, reaching for her phone.

It's interesting that neither of us has thought to text our friends since we started drinking at the airport lounge in Newark.

The front desk clerk is a middle-aged lady with a stunning smile, and she says, "Ohhh, you must be the other beautiful couple we have been expecting." She shakes her head. "Six of the most beautiful guests we have ever had here!"

I put my arm around Roxy's shoulder, and she wraps hers around my waist. "We *are* a beautiful couple, aren't we? See, honey?" I muss up her hair. "She's so insecure about being less attractive than me, but I keep telling her —I'm not out of her league at all."

"Aww, sweetie," she says, patting my chest and grinning at the clerk. "You're in a league all on your own. Nothing will ever change that."

The lady smiles and hands our passports and my credit card back to us, along with two keys and a map of the resort. "You are in the Hibiscus cottage. We are here." She marks an X on the map with a pencil. "Your cottage is here." She circles the Hibiscus cottage with a heart. It is way at the end of a winding path, and if my mind goes to whether or not our friends will be able to hear us should we make any loud noises—well, it can't be helped.

"Ajay will take your luggage to the cottage for you."

When I see the clerk look over my shoulder and swoon a little bit, I know my friends have just walked in.

Sure enough, Matt and Chase are strolling toward us, looking like an underwear model and the lead singer of a grunge band on vacation. They remove their aviator sunglasses at the same time, almost as if they rehearsed it. Roxy sees Bernie and Aimee outside and runs to meet them, patting Matt and Chase on the shoulders as she passes by. The sudden loss of her arm around my waist is surprisingly upsetting.

"Welcome," Matt says to me. "How was your flight?" He's wearing off-white drawstring linen pants and an unbuttoned white shirt with flip flops and a straw panama hat, but he doesn't look the least bit douchey. I hate him.

"How do you already have a tan?"

"I'm from California." He shrugs. "I'm good at tanning."

"'I'm good at tanning.' That's not a thing. I hate you."

He shrugs again, pats me on the arm, and walks back outside to join the women.

Chase lowers his voice and hooks his arm around my neck, only somewhat menacingly. "Getting along with your girlfriend, I see."

"To a degree."

"Which degree would that be?"

"The one that allows for good-humored friendly flirtation and does not involve any form of penetration. Yet."

"You need to rein it in."

"You need to have sex with your wife a couple more times, and then we'll see if you feel the same way about what my dick's up to."

He considers this and releases my neck. "Fair enough."

"I ran into Tamara's brother at the airport," I say as we walk out of the lobby. "She's coming back to New York. By herself. She didn't tell me."

"Sorry, man. You okay? You've moved on, right?"

"Obviously." I glance over at Roxy—but only because she squeals loudly and bounces up and down when she's talking to Aimee and Bernie.

Chase pats me on the back and then picks his wife up, cradling her in his arms. Aimee just grins at him like a horny idiot and kicks her feet up in the air. "We're gonna go Skype with Finn and then figure out a way to pass the time until dinner. See you guys at the restaurant."

Matt and Bernie exchange looks. "Um, we're actually gonna go Skype with Harriet and Daisy now too," Bernie says as she laces her fingers with Matt's. "Unless you want us to have a drink with you at the bar or something?"

Matt is already pulling her down the path away from the common area. "See you guys at dinner!"

And once again, I can practically hear Roxy thinking, "Thanks for leaving me alone with *this* guy."

But she doesn't look annoyed. She removes her shoes and dangles them from her fingers.

"You want to get a drink at the bar?" I ask her.

"No way. I want to see the cottage! Race you there!" She takes off running, passes our friends, and gives me that little smirky look over her shoulder once she's a safe distance away from me.

Oh, don't you worry, honey. I'm coming for you.

The Hibiscus cottage, which is Pepto-Bismol pink on the outside and bright white with glossy dark wood on the inside, is perfect but for one slight problem.

There's no sofa.

Roxy and I are staring at the mosquito-net-covered king-size bed that dominates the room. There are flower petals sprinkled over the top cover. There's a wood bench and one chair in the room. Outside on the veranda, there are two Adirondack chairs, a daybed, a hammock, an infinity plunge pool, and a clawfoot tub.

"Guess we'll have to share the bed," I say, feigning disappointment.

"We can ask for a cot."

I give her a look. "No we can't."

"Why not? Not all couples want to share a bed...You can sleep on the veranda."

"I would get eaten alive by mosquitos."

"I would stab you to death if any part of you touches any part of me in bed."

"I will take that risk. It's a huge bed. There's plenty of room for both of us."

She gives me a look. The fists are on the hips.

"You honestly don't think I can keep my hands off you? You're that irresistible and I'm that much of a horndog?"

Her big gorgeous mouth is sealed shut.

"Or is it *you* that you don't trust around *me*, Miss Carter?"

"Give my regards to the mosquitos, horndog. It's either that or the floor."

We both look down at the shiny dark hardwood floor, and we both know I won't be sleeping on it.

"I hope you realize what a fucking awesome gentleman I'm being by not bringing up the fact that I'm the one paying for this entire vacation."

"I hope you realize how fucking not awesome it is that you just brought it up. And I will pay you for half of everything. I told you I don't need your money."

"And I told you I won't take your money."

"So what are you saying? That *I* should sleep outside?"

"I'm saying that no one should sleep outside."

She is still and quiet and thoughtful for a blissful surprising moment. "We can sleep in four-hour shifts."

"No way. I'm on vacation. I travel internationally, and I have to deal with jet lag all the time. I am not going to mess up my sleep pattern while I'm on vacation in the same time zone as New York. That's not going to happen."

"Fine. I will sleep outside."

"Absolutely not. We'll revisit this again later tonight."

"A higher blood alcohol concentration is not going to affect my decision. I have an extremely high tolerance for alcohol and a very low tolerance for having men in my bed except when they're fucking me." My eyebrows shoot up, and she continues before I can say anything. "Especially if I have no plans to fuck them."

"Interesting choice of words. Plans have a funny way of changing."

She walks past me to the bathroom and says as she shuts the door, "Especially if I have no *desire* to fuck them."

She can't even look at me when she says that because it's a lie.

We will revisit this again later tonight, Foxy Roxy, and it definitely won't be the rum in your system that changes your mind.

When I'm out on the veranda, staring at the amazing sea view, breathing in the amazing warm air, and wondering which one of us is going to take a bath in the outdoor tub first, I hear creaky doors swing open. I turn to see Roxy peering out at me from the bathroom. Or rather —from the walk-in shower.

"The shower opens up onto the veranda!" she says, all excited and almost as if we hadn't been arguing for the past two minutes. "It's like an outdoor shower!"

I'm glad she's excited, because this is the best news I've ever heard.

"This is how you get from the bathroom straight to the outdoor tub!"

"That is so clever and convenient."

"I'm gonna shower before dinner!" she says. "Is that okay?"

"It is beyond okay. Take a shower, take a bath. Whatever you want. I'm going to stand right here. Do your thing."

She narrows her eyes at me and pulls the flimsy wooden doors shut. "Both of the bathroom doors have latches on the inside, FYI."

"I'm going to stand here and enjoy the stunning view of the water and the palm trees and the islands, FYI."

"Good, because that's all you're gonna see!"

Not when I close my eyes, Roxy. You don't even want to know what I see when I close my eyes.

CHAPTER 7
ROXY

don't know why I was expecting dinner to be a fun and casual chatty gathering of the six of us at a big table, but that's what I was expecting.

I should have known all of the tables in the resort's restaurant would be for two.

Matt and Bernadette have already been seated, and the hostess is showing Chase and Aimee to their table.

"Did you want to join us?" Aimee asks me sweetly. "Would it be possible for us to push two tables together?" she asks the hostess.

"No no, it's fine," I say, trying not to mope. "We'll all have drinks at the bar after dinner, yeah?"

"Definitely! Can't wait!"

"*Buon appetito*," Chase says to us as we are ushered to the other side of the open-air room.

Keaton has been strangely silent ever since I emerged from the bathroom in this dress. It's not even a particularly special or revealing dress. I just thought it looked like the kind of thing a gal should wear while on vacation in Antigua. One of the perks of being an executive at an online clothing company is that you get tons of free clothes and accessories, and nobody else at the office was grabbing this breezy chiffon floral-print wrap dress. I didn't realize it had such a high slit until I put it on here. When he saw me, his eyelids fluttered and his jaw tightened, and he just muttered, "That's one helluva dress," and I swear that's the last thing he said. That was fifteen minutes ago.

Then he changed into the kind of cuffed linen trousers that only a guy from Europe or an American dude who invests in hedge funds can get away with. He looks good, sure, and he's got style—yeah. Stylish men can blow me, but I mean, I respect that he knows how to dress.

The hostess stops in front of a table next to the railing, so I can look out at the sunset instead of Keaton's face for an hour at least. Keaton pulls the chair out for me, waits for me to lower my ass to it, and then gently pushes it in toward the table. This is a ridiculous thing that has never happened to me before, so I thank him without thinking about it, but I mean... Of all the traditional gentlemanly gestures, I'd say this is the most useless and we can do without it. It's not like I'm wearing a corset and a ball gown. I am quite capable of seating myself.

"Thank you," I say to him for a second time. "Thank you," I say to the hostess when she hands me the menu. Apparently when I'm stupefied, I just get really polite and improve my posture.

I accidentally glance over at his crotch when he's sitting down across from me. He's definitely wearing boxers, appears to be hanging to the right this evening, and is apparently quite well-endowed. Good for him. He catches me looking and grins. I hold my menu up in front of my face.

Get over yourself, Keaton Bridges. My eyeballs slipped.

"Anya will be your waitress tonight, but can I bring you something fun to drink while you look at our menu?"

Before I can order a beer, Keaton says, "My beautiful girlfriend and I would both love something big, fun, and rum-based. Preferably served in a coconut. With an umbrella."

The hostess smiles. "We have many rum-based drinks, sir, but none of them are served in a coconut, I'm afraid."

"Well, surprise us. Bring us your favorite." He winks at her.

She nods and does a little curtsy before turning and walking away.

"I hate rum," I whisper.

"You'll learn to love it."

"Don't ever order for me again."

"I wouldn't dream of it. I just knew you'd never order a rum drink for yourself, and you need to try it at least once while you're here. Get the full Caribbean experience."

"I'm certainly enjoying island life so far. I think it's safe to say this is the first time I've ever had dinner with a man who wears loafers and no socks."

"Nobody wears socks with loafers."

"It's the first time I've had dinner with a man who wears loafers, I mean."

He leans forward and places his hand on top of mine. "I promise I'll be gentle."

His hand is big and warm, and I slowly slide my hand out from under it because it's way more important for me to vehemently butter my dinner roll than pretend to be his girlfriend at the moment.

I chew angrily while staring at the most breathtaking sunset I have ever seen.

I don't even realize Keaton is taking a picture of me with his phone until he's probably taken a thousand of them. I cover my face. "Hey!"

"I couldn't not take a picture of you with that sunset framing your scowling face."

I scowl at him.

"I'm kidding. You weren't scowling. Look." He holds up his phone and shows me a few of the shots. Surprisingly, I do not look angry at all. I look serene. And pretty. Those may be the best pictures I've seen of myself in ages.

"You're not allowed to post pictures of me on social media."

"Again—I would not dream of it. I'll send them to you. And keep them for my spank bank."

I laugh at that. Because Keaton Bridges saying the words "spank bank" is funny. Not because he's funny.

The hostess returns with two enormous glasses of a coral-colored liquid, each garnished with a giant slice of pineapple and an umbrella. "Caribbean Rum Punch," she says in her deep, sing-song voice. "Pineapple and orange juice, three kinds of rum, fresh lime juice, and grenadine. My favorite and very delicious." She smiles and nods as she places the glass in front of me. "Enjoy!"

Keaton and I both happen to order the same meal, only I manage to order without winking at the waitress, and then I'm left alone with this guy once again.

Keaton holds his glass out to clink against mine, just as I'm about to suck on the straw.

"Oh. Cheers," I say.

"To warm breezes and sunsets and floral dresses with tasteful yet daring slits, and the fine-looking women who wear them."

"To socks and the men who always wear them in public."

He laughs at that. "Whatever, Socksy Roxy."

"Is that my new nickname?"

"Nope. That's just what I'm calling you right now because I'm so witty."

This cocktail goes down smooth, and it's not too sweet at all. I smack my lips together. It tastes even more fun than the margaritas at TGI Fridays. "I like it. The rum punch. Not the nickname."

"It's not your nickname, and I knew you would. Tell me about your family."

"No. This isn't a date."

"Tell me about your vagina, then."

"What?"

"You wouldn't tell a guy about your vagina on a date, would you?"

"What kind of logic is that?"

"We don't have to talk at all if you don't want to." He shrugs and looks out at the sunset.

"Okay, fine. My parents' names are Joe and Melinda Carter. My dad's a mechanic, and my mom's an office manager. They live in Baltimore. They've always lived in Baltimore. I have a brother named Paul who lives in Canada with his wife and three dogs."

"What kind of a mechanic?"

"He restores classic cars."

"Really? What's his specialty?"

"Corvettes. Second and third generation."

"From the sixties."

"Yes. You know about Corvettes?"

"I have a passing knowledge. My best friend from high school, his dad collected them. Still does, I guess. Sting Rays."

"Yeah, '65 is his favorite year. And '63 of course, but he doesn't get to work on many of those in Baltimore."

"I once saw a beautiful white '65 Corvette convertible in the Hamptons. Maroon interior. Teakwood steering wheel."

"Ermine white. Yeah, my dad restored one of those. I helped him with that one, actually, when I was like sixteen."

"You helped your dad restore cars?"

"Sometimes. I know my way around a lug nut."

"That isn't arousing at all."

"Most men are totally turned off by the notion."

"I'm definitely not picturing you in cutoffs and a tiny T-shirt, covered in grease."

"Good, because I was working with my dad, so that would be really inappropriate."

"Right."

"I wore coveralls. With nothing underneath."

He chokes on his rum drink.

"You okay over there?"

"We don't have to talk anymore."

"Oh, but I want to hear about *your* family."

"I don't feel like talking about my family."

"Is that allowed?"

"You didn't have to talk about your family if you didn't want to."

"That's annoying."

"Why? We had a nice little conversation about Corvettes and garage porn. I feel so much closer to you now."

"I'm so happy for the local mosquitos. They're gonna feast tonight."

"What would you like to talk about?"

"We don't have to talk about anything."

"You're a really fun date."

"It's not a date."

"What kind of office does your mother manage?"

"An ophthalmology practice."

"Interesting. Your parents sound like they might be a little different."

"From you? Very."

"From each other."

"A little. I mean, I guess they used to be, but they've, you know. Merged. Over the years."

"Interesting."

THE PLUS ONES 91

"They have fun together."

"How?"

"You want to know how my parents have fun together?"

"We don't have to talk at all if you really don't want to."

We sit in silence for one terrible everlasting minute. He grins at me, and I fidget, and he's amused by my fidgeting, and fuck this guy. "They just have fun with each other. Like all the time, doing anything. They tease each other and make each other laugh. They make up these stupid card games that only they know the rules to."

"Do they let other people play with them?"

"No. It's their own thing. I mean, they have their own game that's called Poker? I Don't Even Know Her! but they made up another game for Paul and me and they refused to give it a name, we'd just call it The Card Game."

"Did they make up the rules as you went along?"

"No. The rules were very clear and pretty simple." I describe the rules in great detail, as well as my favorite memory of the time we all played it on Christmas Eve at my grandparents' house. I get teary-eyed and shift around in my chair and then polish off my Caribbean Rum Punch. "I can't believe I just told you all that. How much rum did they put in this thing?" I say.

"It's not the rum," he says. "That card game's called Spades, by the way. You were playing Spades."

"No. It's a card game that my parents made up for us."

"Okay. You get along with your brother?"

"Yes. Why? You think I have a problem with all men? I don't. It's just you."

"So I'm special?"

"You are uniquely infuriating."

"You are highly sensitive to my uniquely infuriating qualities."

"We're oil and water."

He starts choking on his rum punch again.

Was it something I said? "You okay over there, sweetie?"

He gives me the thumbs-up and finally stops coughing. When he catches his breath, he says, "What we have is friction. Oil and water just glide right past each other." He clenches his jaw for a second before continuing. "I'm more like a match that's striking against your rough surface. Creating sparks. Producing a flame. Lighting you up."

"Rubbing me the wrong way."

"Just tell me how you like it, sweetie." He winks. "I aim to please."

Thank God the waitress comes over with our dinner, because it feels like someone spilled a little oil and water in my panties and I am done bantering with this guy. No good can come of this.

Keaton looks over his shoulder at Chase and Aimee and at Matt and Bernadette. They—and the rest of the diners in this restaurant—are in their own little happy couple bubbles. I watch him. The way he looks at them —it's breaking my heart a little. He's filled with longing. Not for them, although maybe it's a little bit about that, but mostly for what they have. It takes me back to that moment with him on the deck, the night of the wedding.

But I can't go back there.

We can't go back there.

It was lovely, but ultimately all it did was create even more of a barrier between us. For me, anyway. For whatever reason.

"Are you going to call Tamara?" I blurt out. I don't know why. I don't really care one way or another, I just need to talk about something other than him rubbing me or how in love our friends are.

He slowly turns back to face me and then picks up his fork to poke at the chicken medallions. He considers the question before answering, which is not something I'm used to with Keaton. He's more of a snappy comeback kind of guy. "No. I'm not going to call her... There's a Russian word. *Razbliuto.* It's the sentimental feeling you have about someone you once loved. Someone you don't love anymore. That's what I have for her. It's not even her that I miss, really. It's being in love. Having someone to love. Being allowed to love someone."

I swallow hard and take a sip of water before clearing my throat and saying, "Yeah, I know the feeling." I really do. But it's not something I'm going to talk about with Keaton.

Every now and then, I realize why Chase has been best friends with this guy since college. It's a mystery to me most of the time, and then all of a sudden, I get this glimpse into the fascinating world beneath the manscaped tailored privileged Upper East Side golden boy on the surface—the one I want to dropkick. I don't want to explore that world, but I like knowing it's there. For Chase and Aimee and Finn's sake.

We're mostly quiet for the rest of the meal, and it's okay. It's not awkward silence. It's nice, even. It's the kind of comfortable silence that fills a space between two people, maybe not with love or longing or even friendship but with something that doesn't need a word or a label in any language.

CHAPTER 8
KEATON

Drinks at the bar after dinner lasted all of thirty minutes before the married people claimed they needed to go back to their cottages to get a good night's sleep. As if we aren't all adults and friends who know perfectly well they're going to be boning until the wee small hours of the morning. I think they just don't want Roxy and me to feel awkward. Until dinner tonight, I didn't think it was possible for Roxy Carter to feel awkward about anything, but she just couldn't take the silence until I gave her an answer about Tamara.

"I was really hoping for *samar*," I say as Roxy and I watch the four of them meander, arm-in-arm, up the path to the cottages.

"Who's Samar?" she asks, finishing her cocktail.

"It's not a who, it's a what. It's an Arabic term. There's no English equivalent. It means staying up late and having a good time with loved ones. The kind of conversations you only have with good friends at night. When you don't even realize what time it is because you're so happy to be relaxing and figuring out the meaning of life with the people who matter the most to you. And getting really drunk, usually."

I watch her swallow the last of her second rum punch as she digests the meaning of the word *samar,* and I know it's what she wanted too. It's what we've been missing. It's why we're here. A warm mist obscures the ice blue of her eyes for one brief second, and then it vanishes like a mirage. She obviously does not want to experience *samar* with me. "What are you—a linguist? And don't say you're a very cunning linguist, because I'm afraid if I roll my eyes one more time today they'll stay that way."

"I actually minored in linguistics at Wharton."

She snorts, very lady-like. "A sentence only ever uttered by men who wear loafers with no socks."

"Did you just say the word 'uttered' out loud? You're so pretentious."

She can't help but grin at that callback. "You're right. I meant 'spewed.'"

"Anyway, I had a linguistics professor who'd write an untranslatable word on the chalkboard at the beginning of every class. I started keeping a separate notebook with those words and their meanings in it. Still have it."

"Was she hot? The professor?"

"Yes. I'm a simple man."

She cocks her head to one side and studies my face. "Are you, though?"

"No, I'm not."

She blinks and shakes her head and then hops down off the bar stool, and I just happen to notice and praise the

Lord that it makes her tits bounce a little. Roxy does not want to stay at the bar to have another drink with me while discussing whether or not I am a simple man, and she definitely doesn't want to provide me with any more opportunities to see her glorious tits jiggle in that fantastic dress. She declines my invitation to go for a walk on the beach or anywhere else on the property, she most certainly does not want to check out the live music and dancing, and she also does not want to join the other guests in the lobby for Game Night. It's like as soon as I made the comment about *samar*, she decided she just wanted the night to be over so she can start the day tomorrow with Aim and Bernie. I get it. It's fine. She doesn't want to fall madly in love with me, and she's clearly in danger of doing just that.

So here we are, back in the Hibiscus Cottage. She doesn't want to take a dip in the plunge pool, she doesn't want either one of us taking a candlelit bath, and there's no TV in the room, so I'm on the veranda trying to Face-Time with my dog. And she's wearing an oversize T-shirt and pajama pants while reading in bed.

"Is the volume turned up on your iPad?" I ask the caretaker at the dog hotel.

"It's up all the way," she assures me. "He can definitely hear you."

That would explain why he's just lying there in his bed, staring at the wall.

"Hey, buddy. You miss me? You having fun? Jackpot. Jackpot. Jackpot...Okay, he seems tired. Or is he depressed?"

"No, he's been in really good spirits all day. I think

maybe he's worn out from playing so much." She's not a very good liar, but I do appreciate the effort.

"Sure. Okay, then. Thank you. I'll check in tomorrow. Good night. Good night, Jackpot." I end the video call. *Asshole.* I step back inside the room. "You want me to leave the doors open for a while?"

"No, you can close them. I'm actually kind of tired," Roxy says, yawning, closing her book, and placing it on the bedside table. "I'm gonna try to sleep."

It's nine forty-five.

It's interesting to me that she's on the left side of the bed, since I prefer the right.

"Sure. Would you mind if I listen to music with my headphones while I do a little work on my laptop? I can go back outside for a bit."

"Go right ahead," she says, fluffing up her pillow. "Good night."

"Good night."

We haven't revisited the topic of discussion from earlier, so I'd like to think that since she hasn't told me to stay outside all night, I will assume that she has realized it will be no big deal for me to sleep in the same bed as her. She turns off the bedside lamp, lays her head back against the downy pillow, and crosses her arms over her chest, closing her eyes.

She looks so pretty with no makeup and no tension in her face.

"Stop looking at me," she says, her eyes still closed.

"I'm looking for my headphones," I say. They're right there with my laptop, of course. I pick them up and go back out onto the veranda, get comfortable in one of the

Adirondack chairs, and fire up my Jay-Z playlist. It's what I listen to when I'm analyzing financial data. It works for me. It's how I get into my flow state.

Two minutes into "99 Problems," and I think I scream loud enough to wake people up in Florida when a hand slaps the back of my head. I nearly sprain my neck turning back to see Roxy standing behind me with her fists on her hips. I pull my headphones off. "What?"

"I can hear your music."

"Why didn't you close the doors?"

"I did. I could still hear it. I have very good ears."

"I'll turn it down."

"Can you listen to something with a little less bass?"

"No."

"Can you work on your laptop without listening to music?"

I take a deep breath and exhale slowly. I don't want to piss her off because I want to sleep in that bed. "Sure. I can do that." I turn off Jay-Z and place my phone and the headphones on the floor.

"Fantastic. Thank you."

"Sorry to disturb."

She stomps back over to the bed, and I watch her get in and get settled. "Stop watching me."

"Okay."

I turn back to my laptop. I can work to the sound of the waves lapping against the shore, no problem. I get back into my flow state again. I'm typing up notes and writing an email to my business manager when I hear Roxy say in a deep voice, "I can hear you typing."

"I'll try to type more quietly."

"I'll still be able to hear it."

"I can assure you I'm very good at getting the job done with the gentle touch of my fingertips."

"I can promise you it will still piss me off. I'm a light sleeper."

"You're not even asleep yet."

"Exactly."

I sigh and save my work, close the laptop. "Guess I'll try to sleep too then. I hope the sound of me brushing my teeth doesn't rattle you too much."

"Just get it over with," she grumbles.

"That's what she said."

"I'll bet she did."

When I take my pajamas and travel pouch into the bathroom, my first thought is that I should call the front desk to let them know we've been burglarized. There are towels on the floor and half of a Sephora store spread out haphazardly over the entire two-sink marble counter. I turn to look back at Roxy, who appears so innocent lying there, but she is clearly a madwoman, because who the fuck does this to a beautiful luxury bathroom and then doesn't clean up after herself?

I guess she hears me moving a few of her beauty products, because she yells out, "Don't touch my stuff!"

"I need to make room for *my* stuff."

"Well, don't touch my stuff."

"Would you like to come in here and move your stuff for me? Because I think that would be a great idea."

The door is closed, but I swear I can hear her whispering "fuck you" and I'm sure she's flipping me the double bird right now. But she doesn't come to help me tidy up, so I guess I'll be doing it for her. I line all of the bottles and containers and brushes and tubes up as neatly and quietly as possible, pick up the towels, because that's driving me nuts, and finally get around to brushing my teeth.

"Oh my God! Of course you would have an electric toothbrush!"

I don't respond, because that would just be more noise.

This is a delightful side of Roxy Carter and such a wonderful surprise.

I continue to brush through the four beeps and until my electric toothbrush automatically shuts off. I rinse my mouth with less vigor than I normally would and cleanse my face with as little splashing as possible. When I'm done with the face cloth, I fold and hang it back exactly the way I found it, and then I change into my pajamas. I fucking hate wearing pajamas, but I knew she wouldn't want to share a bed with me if I'm just wearing boxers.

You'd think a woman who's as comfortable as she clearly is with sex would be a lot more laid-back about being around a man in private. I take one last look at that shower. She is being exactly the opposite of Oiled-up Shower Roxy tonight. Which is probably a good thing. For now.

I am so fucking thoughtful, I even turn off the bathroom light before opening the door so she doesn't complain about that too. The sky is so clear and the moonlight is so bright I can see perfectly. I fold up my clothes and place them over my suitcase and then climb into bed like a ninja. I don't even disturb the flower petals that are still lying on top of the cover. She doesn't say anything, so I'm staying.

She's still lying on her back, but I lie on my side with my back to her, and I'm practically lined-up with the edge of the mattress. I can do this. I can sleep like this. She barely even smells like cocoa butter anymore. I'm barely even thinking about sixteen-year-old Roxy bending over an engine under the hood of a Corvette in a tiny T-shirt and cutoffs.

Just as the sweet mistress of sleep is about to embrace me to her bosom, I am startled by what is surely the sound of a wild boar that has snuck into our cottage. I slowly turn over and hike myself up onto my elbow to discover—to my horror and delight—that my bedmate is snoring. *Roxy Carter snores.* It's not an adorable little rhythmic quiver like a purring cat. It's like when a fighter jet flies right overhead and everything rattles, only this jet is filled with angry barnyard animals and a sloppy drumline.

I can't explain why this makes me so happy, but it does.

"Roxy," I say. I don't reach over to touch her, because I totally believe she'd stab me if I did, but I keep saying her name over and over until she finally stirs.

When she opens her eyes, she is understandably confused to see me, and when she realizes I'm laughing at her, she is understandably annoyed. *"What?"*

"You're snoring."

"What? Shut up. I wasn't even asleep."

"You shut up. You were asleep. And you were snoring. Really loud."

"I don't snore."

"Oh, but you do."

"That's not possible."

"You honestly think I'm lying about this? Why would I?"

"Why would I snore?"

"I don't think you're doing it on purpose."

"Well...was it like a quiet little snore, like I have a stuffed nose or something?"

"Have you ever heard Daisy the dog snore?"

"Yeah, it's sweet."

"What you were doing was nothing like that. It was like lying next to an erupting volcano."

She laughs. "I still don't believe you."

"Try sleeping on your side."

"I don't want to sleep on my side. My mom's been sleeping on her side her whole life, and now she has wrinkly skin on her chest."

"Does she snore?"

"I don't think so."

"How long have your parents been married?"

"Almost forty years."

"And you're not even willing to try sleeping on your side for one night?"

"Believe it or not, I am not trying to maintain a forty-year marriage to you."

"Yet."

"Hah."

"It's probably just because of the alcohol. You drank a lot today. And by the way, you really are quite adept at holding your liquor. I'm impressed."

"Told you."

"But it makes you snore."

"I just don't see how that's possible."

"No one's ever told you that you snore before?"

"No. I told you I don't like sleeping with guys."

"But you lived with Aimee."

"Yeah, in college. And not even for a whole year in Brooklyn, thanks to Chase. But she didn't actually sleep in my room."

"How long has it been since you slept in the same bed or the same room with a guy?"

"Years."

"So you really don't date, do you? What's your deal? You just hang out with dudes and have sex with them and that's it?"

"Please go outside."

"Okay, no more talking. But no more snoring either."

"I don't snore."

"Okay. But maybe the reason you're such a light sleeper is you keep waking yourself up with the snoring. Just a theory. So I'm the first guy you've slept in the same bed with in how many years?"

"I can't sleep with someone else in my bed. At all. Ever."

"Well, you were obviously sleeping before, unless you snore when you're awake."

"I don't snore."

"Okay. You're really not going to try sleeping on your side?"

She huffs and flips over so her back is to me. I watch as her breathing slows. I wonder if her nipples are still erect. They've been on high alert all day long. They must be exhausted.

"Stop looking at me."

"Good night." I turn over onto my other side. I know why it makes me happy that she snores. It's because it makes her seem like more of a real person and less of a hot chick from a video game.

Five minutes later, she's asleep and snoring, and I'm holding my phone over her head, recording this amazing noise as a voice memo. I really want to use the camera so I can prove that it's her, but that just seems creepy. I also really want to wake her up again so I can play this back to her, but it's probably a dick move to wake her up twice just to prove a point. I stop recording and place my phone back on the bedside table.

It takes an hour of lying here listening to Roxy snoring before I realize that I can put on my headphones and hope that they block out the sound. I lie on my back with the headphones on for another half an hour or so, unable to fall asleep because I'm so amused by the fact that she snores *and* that she's able to sleep so soundly with me in the same bed as her. She isn't going to believe one of those things in the morning, but she'll wake up with a better idea of just how special Keaton Bridges really is to her.

CHAPTER 9
KEATON

t's after ten when I get to the breakfast buffet. I woke up to an empty room, a note that said ***The headphones are a bit much***, and a multitude of group texts telling me that everyone else was eating breakfast two hours ago. Now, everyone else is already at the pool, but Chase is being an actual best friend for a change, and he has come over to keep me company while I eat and guzzle coffee.

"She snores? Really?"

"I would have had a better night's sleep if I'd shared a bed with Godzilla. I could still hear it with the head-phones on."

"Well, she's in an awfully good mood this morning."

"I'll bet. She must have slept really well."

"And not because..." He dips down to get me to look him in the eyes.

I look at him straight on. "Definitely not because..."

"I don't believe she snores. Really?"

I tap the voice memo on my phone. If she's going to

leave me alone in the room while she has breakfast with our friends, then I am going to share the astonishing sound of her airway tissues vibrating with them.

"Holy shit." Chase covers his mouth and laughs. "That sounds fake."

"If it was, then I'd better have a talk with her to clarify exactly what it is she's supposed to be faking while we're here."

"So...you're totally turned-off now, then?"

I sigh. "No."

"Because I gotta warn you. We're all hanging out at the pool."

"And?"

"And she's wearing a bikini and you need to keep it together."

I look down at my half-eaten breakfast and place my fork on the plate. "I think I'm done."

"I'm serious. You need to mentally prepare yourself. I mean, Matt and I have our gorgeous wives to look at, but you should probably stare directly at the sun or something."

I laugh. "Okay." I pat him on the back. "If you're trying to talk it up so I'll be disappointed, I think you've done an admirable job."

Chase shakes his head and puts his sunglasses on. "I do not envy you. You are in for a world of pain, my friend. Don't say I didn't warn you."

When we arrive poolside, Aimee and Bernie are dangling their feet into the water and Matt and all twenty of his abs are lying out on a chaise lounge. Fucking asshole. Where's the dad bod? He squints up at me. "Hey, man. Nice of you to join us."

"Yo, Keats!" Bernie lifts her chin at me. "We were just about to come get you."

"Roxy said you had a hard time getting to sleep last night," Aimee says.

"Did she? I don't suppose she mentioned *why* that was..." I am momentarily distracted by the stunning view of the bougainvillea and the beach and the sea and the sailboats and the sky, but all of a sudden, I wish I had taken Chase's advice about staring directly into the sun.

A slim figure cuts through the center of the crystal-clear water in the infinity pool, and then everything that isn't that slim figure just fades away.

There's that Phoebe Cates pool scene in *Fast Times at Ridgemont High* that I jerked off to a thousand times between the ages of twelve and twelve and a half, and then there's this Roxy Carter pool scene that I will be jerking it to for the rest of my godforsaken life.

She ascends the steps at the side of the pool, glistening wet and carefully adjusting the top and bottom of her black bikini to ensure that nothing that isn't supposed to be exposed to the good people of Antigua and its tourists are showing, but it hardly matters because what *is* exposed is the most gorgeous toned but curvy body I have ever seen in the flesh. And I've dated women who look good for a living. But there's just something about Roxy Carter that screams sex to me.

I mean, Roxy Carter herself may be screaming "I'm not having sex with you" to me over and over again, but methinks the lady doth protest too much, and also I can't hear what anyone's saying because all I hear is "Moving in Stereo" by The Cars and every cell in my body is muttering *fuuuuuuuuck* and covering its lap with a textbook.

And that's just when I'm getting the view of her backside. When she turns and starts walking in my direction, I realize that my sunglasses have actually started to fog up a little. So I remove them, and I do not bother to hide that I am staring at her magnificent perky tits in that triangle bikini top, because it's her fault that my brain is barely functioning this morning and my reaction time is a little slow and because I do not want to stop staring.

"Morning, sleepyhead," she says as she walks right past me to pick up the towel that's lying on the chaise lounge right next to me.

I would kill myself right now if I was guaranteed to be immediately reincarnated as that towel. "Uh-huh."

"You get breakfast?"

"I did. Thank you for your concern."

"You should go for a swim—in half an hour, of course. The water's amazing."

"Of course. I intend to."

"You just gonna stand there like a narc?" she asks while obnoxiously toweling off every inch of her amazing body.

"Actually..." I say as I pull my phone out from my pocket, "I'm going to stand here and listen to this." I tap the voice memo and point the speaker in her direction. Because this phone and that recording are the only things keeping me from dropping to my knees and begging her to marry me right now.

The expression of shock and horror on her face do nothing to make her look any less gorgeous and sexy, but at least I'm getting some kind of a reaction from her. She covers her mouth. "Shut up."

"I wish you could have."

"Oh my God! There must be something wrong with me!"

Not that I can see.

"Turn it off! Turn it off!"

I turn it off.

"Oh no! I'm so sorry. Keaton! Why didn't you wake me up?"

"You're kidding, right?"

"You should have woken me up."

"You would have murdered me."

"I can't believe you didn't try to smother me with a pillow."

"I don't think it would have helped. Maybe don't drink so much alcohol today. See if that changes things."

She laughs. "I'll do my best to abstain. Oh my God. Keaton, I'm really sorry."

"It's okay." Actually, it's so much worse now that she's actually being nice about it.

She finishes drying herself off, then arranges her towel on top of the chaise lounge, and then arranges herself on top of the towel. She puts her sunglasses on and looks around at Aimee and Bernie, who are snuggling up to their husbands. Finally, she reaches down into her beach bag, pulls out a bottle of sunscreen, and glances up at me. "Um, would you mind getting my back?" she asks almost apologetically.

I take the sunscreen from her. If this is her way of apologizing for last night, then I accept. Ohhhhh, I accept. I can't form words right now, but *yes.*

She scooches forward to make room for me on the chaise lounge behind her. I take in a deep breath and situate myself so that I have full access to the backside of her upper body. I sweep the ends of her damp hair over one shoulder. She reaches back to hold her hair up, and our fingers touch for a brief electric moment. I use my fingertip to swipe a few stray hairs away, and I can't help but note the way she shivers.

She clears her throat. "If you could get to it before the sun goes down, that would be great."

"You want this done right or not?"

"There's no wrong way to apply sunscreen to someone's back."

"There's a right way to do it when the right guy is doing it."

She guffaws. "Okay, let's not turn this into a thing."

I squeeze a quarter-size amount of the lotion onto the palm of my hand. It smells like cocoa butter and sex and being slowly castrated by my best friend, who's watching me from twenty feet away. *Fuck him*—I would gladly sacrifice both balls for this woman. I place my hand flat on her back between her shoulder blades and stroke slowly in an upward circular motion. Her skin is smooth and warm and alive beneath my hand, and I just need three hours alone with her in our cottage and then I'm done.

I apply more lotion to her shoulders and the back of her neck, almost up to her hairline, and then I drag my fingers down her spine to unhook the bra hook closure, quickly, before she can protest. She gasps and lets her hair drop back down, using her hands to hold the front of her bikini in place.

"No one's lookin' but me, darlin', and I can only see your back."

She shifts around, stretches her legs out straight in front of her, and I can't see it, but I know she's squeezing her thighs together.

There's a right way to do this, Roxy Carter, and I'm doing it to you right now.

I use both hands to massage the sunscreen into her lower back and hips until she groans quietly, realizes she just groaned, straightens up, and says, "Okay, I think I'm good." She swallows hard.

"You need me to get the backs of your legs?"

"Nope. Thanks."

I fasten the clasp on her back, make sure everything's in place, and wipe my hands on her towel. "You're welcome."

I need to get out of here before I start singing "Your Body is a Wonderland" and weeping.

I stand up and remove my shirt, stretch my arms up in the air. I don't hear anyone applauding, but I just need a good hour or two of sun, and then I'll be golden. Literally. "Think I'll go for a walk on the beach."

"Are you wearing sunscreen?" Because of the sunglasses, I can't see the hearts in her eyes as she checks out my naked torso, but I'm confident that they're there.

"No. I'll be fine."

"Absolutely not, young man. Get back down here."

She grabs the bottle of sunscreen, bends her knees, and signals for me to take a seat in front of her, but no.

Nope.

Just. No.

I'm getting out of here while I still have the upper hand.

I would rather risk a sunburn than risk trying to kiss her and blurting out "I love you" while she caresses my shoulders.

"I'm good," I say. "Thanks, though."

I walk away, down to the beach, leaving her wanting more, leaving myself with a little dignity and a semi that is nobody's business but my own.

CHAPTER 10
ROXY

diot.

He's a fairly adorable idiot, but an idiot, none-theless.

I told him he needed sunscreen, but he didn't listen, and now my fake boyfriend is moping at the cottage with bright-pink shoulders.

I'm standing at the bar of the restaurant with Aimee. The four of them are going to have lunch here, but I'm ordering takeout for two. For myself and my idiot fake boyfriend. He's got good hands and he knows how to use them, but his brain is just not working today. That may be my fault, and I might feel a tiny bit guilty about it.

"We're going to check out the live band and go dancing after dinner tonight," Aimee says. "Before Game Night. You're coming to that, right?"

I wrinkle my nose. "Game Night, sure, but probably not the dancing."

Aimee gives me a knowing look. "It's not *that* kind of dancing."

"That's not why I don't want to go." I'm not a good dancer, okay? You'd think I would be, because you know —good on the dance floor equals good in bed, right? And I'm good in bed. But for some reason I've never progressed beyond that Junior High-Molly Ringwald-in-*The Breakfast Club* kind of dance move. Aimee saw it in college, and I've managed to avoid all potential dance-related situations since then. And I will be avoiding this situation because I do not need to be sharing a bed *and* dirty dancing with Keaton Bridges.

"Okay," she says, even though she totally thinks I'm just embarrassed about how I dance, but that is not it. "But you'll definitely come to Game Night? It should be fun."

"What is it, Charades or something?"

"I'm not sure exactly. Couples games? Teams?"

"Greeeaaaat."

"You guys really do look cute together," she says.

I scoff at that. "Sure we do."

"You do. For what it's worth." She shrugs.

I bite my lower lip and then say, "He ran into Tamara's brother at the airport yesterday."

"I know. Chase told me. Poor guy."

"You think he's still hung up on her?"

She shakes her head. "No. Definitely not. I just think it's a blow to his ego. He needs someone else to focus his energy on. He's really sweet."

He actually is, isn't he?

"If you say so."

Aimee smacks her lips together and says, "So you guys are just going to hang in your room for a while?"

"Yeah, I'm gonna see if they have any aloe vera at the front desk or something."

"For Keaton?"

"Yeah."

"Awww, Roxy. That's sweet."

"No it isn't. It's not anything."

"Okay." She grins. "If you say so."

I carry our picnic basket of takeout food, dishes, and cutlery, going by the front desk on my way back. "Keaton already has a sunburn," I say, rolling my eyes.

The lady points out all of the aloe vera plants that grow along the sides of the path and in the garden beds around the property. "You are welcome to them. But here, take this for your boyfriend," she says, handing me a big, plump aloe leaf that has already had the serrated edges and the top skin removed.

I giggle, for no reason other than it's so funny to hear Keaton referred to as my boyfriend. Giggling is stupid, and I've done it so many times since yesterday. I'm not even tipsy right now.

I can hear Keaton moaning from outside the front door, and not in a sexy way.

"I'm back, you big baby."

He is lying facedown on the bed. He looks up at me and winces. "It hurts when I turn my neck."

"I brought lunch. And aloe vera."

"Aloe vera?"

"Yeah, it's fresh. For your sunburn."

He grunts. "Thanks," he says into the mattress. "I'll do it."

"Do what?"

"Apply it to my shoulders."

"You just said it hurts to move your neck."

"I can do it," he insists, lying completely still and facedown.

I place the picnic basket on the floor and straddle his back before he even knows what hit him. I hear another muffled grunt, but he doesn't move. I let the exposed, gooey side of the leaf glide across the skin of his shoulders and upper back. He groans, in the good way. When there's enough gel on his skin, I gently rub it around with my fingertips.

He's in better shape than I thought he would be. He isn't all bulked-up or anything, but he isn't soft either. He takes care of himself. I wouldn't exactly say I can't handle his shirtlessness, but he ain't bad to look at. Or touch.

"Feel better?"

He lets out a quiet moan. His arms are stretched out straight along his sides, and when I'm moving around to climb off him, his fingers graze my calves. I can't tell if he did it on purpose or not, but it felt good. I hop off the bed.

"You want to eat, or do you need to sleep?"

"Mmmph" is his answer.

"Okay, well, it's a sandwich, so you can eat it later."

I eat my sandwich on the daybed out on the veranda. I could use a nap myself, but I decide to text my parents to ask them if The Card Game they "invented" for me and my brother is actually Spades.

MOM: Who told you?

DAD: Took you long enough to figure it out, hon.

ME: You said you made it up for Paul and me!

MOM: <shrugging woman emoji> We wanted you guys to think that you were special and that we were creative parents. Who told you?

ME: No one.

MOM: Well, we can't wait to hear more about him.

ME: I'm in Antigua right now, btw.

DAD: Where?!

ME: The Caribbean. With Aimee and her husband and a few other friends. It's a group vacation thing. It's gorgeous here.

MOM: Roxanne, are you there with a boy?!

ME: Nope. Gotta go! Love you!

DAD: He sounds like trouble to me.

MOM: You say that about all the boys.

DAD: And I'm right every time.

MOM: Don't listen to him! Have fun. Oh hey, Dad, bring me the big red salad bowl from the dining table.

DAD: Where is it?

MOM: On the dining table. In the dining room.

DAD: I don't see it.

MOM: OMG never mind. I'll get it.

ME: You guys. Stop.

MOM: Oh sorry, dear! Have fun!

DAD: Not too much fun.

When I wake up from the nap that I didn't mean to take and the sex dream that I did not mean to have, Keaton is standing nearby, saying my name quietly, over and over again. Just like he did last night and sort of like he was doing in my sex dream just now but without all the heavy breathing.

"Hey."

"Hi," I say, rubbing my eyes and trying to look like someone who totally was not just dreaming about getting plowed by him. "Your shoulders feel better?"

"They really do. I can move and everything. That stuff is magic. Thank you."

"Good. You're welcome."

"Everyone's heading down for dinner now. You wanna go? They're going dancing after."

I sit up. "Actually, I still have half a sandwich. I'm not that hungry. Did you want to go? To the restaurant, I mean. I mean, you can go dancing too, if you want. I'm not going to."

"Why not?"

I shrug. "I hate dancing."

"Who hates dancing?"

"I do."

"That's insane."

"If you say so."

"So you just want to hang out with me in the room for a couple of hours before we go to Game Night?"

"No. I want to hang out in the room for a couple of hours, and you can do whatever you want to do."

He smiles and shakes his head, looking out at the water and probably wishing he'd brought someone else. "Okay," he says. "I want to get into this plunge pool. Naked."

"Go nuts," I say, getting up. "I'll be inside. Eating a sandwich and not watching you."

"Whatever you want."

"That's what I want."

"You're welcome to join me."

"I won't, but thanks."

I don't close the doors to the veranda when I go inside, but I do close the curtains.

It's not my fault that the curtains are so lightweight and it's definitely not my fault that it's so breezy right now, but I do take full responsibility for staring at Keaton's naked butt when he jumps into the plunge pool, because—*dayum*. It is surprisingly fine.

Damn that rich white ass.

CHAPTER 11
KEATON

"It's a paper—that movie about the newspaper! The one with the Catholics! The one that made me cry!"

"You're supposed to actually name the title of the movie, Bernie," I remind her.

Matt is very slowly and carefully drawing what looks like a book on the dry erase board, while quickly drawing out his wife's crazy.

"Oh, it's a book!" Bernie yells out.

Matt points at her and calmly says, "Yes."

"*The Notebook!*"

Matt shakes his head and signals for her to keep going.

"That actress from *The Notebook* who was in that movie about the newspaper and the Catholics!"

He keeps pointing at the book and signals for her to keep guessing.

"It's a movie that's based on a book? Harry Potter!"

Everyone in the hotel lobby is quietly laughing.

"Give me more clues, oh my God!"

Matt just ignores Bernie while he draws another perfect rectangle on the board. Meanwhile, there's fifteen seconds left on the timer.

"It's another piece of paper. Draw faster!"

The rectangle slowly becomes an upright box. Matt draws a perfect circle on it and points to it.

"It's a ball in a box. It's—a milk carton?"

Matt signals to her to keep going and keeps pointing at the circle.

"It's—it's a carton—a carton of orange juice!"

"Yes!" He draws little dots beside the orange and then points to the orange.

"Orange juice—fruit flies. Pulp? *Pulp Fiction!*"

"Time!" the resort manager calls out just as Matt jumps up and punches the air and then high-fives his wife, picks her up, and twirls her around. I don't think I've ever seen him this animated, and also—holy shit—how did they do that? They were a total disaster, and then all of a sudden—bam. It's like they were reading each other's minds or Matt just knew that she'd get it eventually.

I exchange a look with Roxy. We're up after Chase and Aimee, who are up after these guys, but Matt and Bernie get to keep going and switching off until they blow it. We've been watching other couples play Couples Pictionary for the past half an hour—or Couples Win, Lose, or Draw, as Don and Debbie prefer to call it. They're the oldest couple here, and they went five rounds to win ten points before failing when Don couldn't figure out *Taxi Driver*. They nearly got into a brawl over it.

It's fun, but there's an undercurrent of real competitiveness because the prize is a free couples massage, and who wouldn't want that?

Bernie thoroughly erases the upright dry erase board, stretches her fingers, and cracks her neck before reaching into the box to pull out an index card with a movie title on it. She looks very excited, narrows her eyes at her husband, and then says, "Got it!" The big timer gets reset to a one-minute countdown, and Bernie starts to draw...or paint. She's holding the marker like a paintbrush and doing big strokes and shading.

Matt's just leaning back in the sofa and grinning at his wife, waiting for her to complete her masterpiece. "It's a mountain."

"Yes!" She signals for him to keep guessing.

"*Cold Mountain.*"

She shakes her head and continues drawing something in front of the mountain.

"*Brokeback Mountain.*"

She shakes her head.

"*Cliffhanger.*"

She shakes her head and quickly draws what is clearly a woman with her arms outstretched. She points to the woman and then to the mountain and then draws circles and arrows around the woman.

"It's a woman and a mountain."

She smiles and signals for him to keep going but then adds more details to the woman and the mountain. She is a professional painter, so she takes this part of the game very seriously. Meanwhile, all of her friends are laughing at her. She keeps drawing circles around the smiling woman.

"A mountain woman? *Misery*."

She shakes her head and glares at him.

"Are you sure it's not *Cold Mountain*?"

"Time!"

"Oh my God!" Bernie yells at Matt. "*The Sound of Music!*"

Aimee and Roxy are dying laughing.

"I literally drew the movie poster! That's Julie Andrews singing and spinning around on a hill in front of the Alps!"

Matt doesn't even move when she smacks him on the arm. "Why didn't you just draw an ear and a musical note?"

"Because that's not pretty," she says, her lower lip sticking out.

Matt pulls her onto his lap. "That's a beautiful drawing, babe."

"Okay! Very good! One point for Matt and Bernadette!" says the resort manager. "Up next is Mr. Chase and Mrs. Aimee!"

We clap and hoot and holler. Chase gets up to erase the board as Aimee rubs her hands together. She decides to stand up for this. "Pick a good one, baby!"

"We got this," Chase says as he picks out an index card and looks at it for half a second and then nods and goes to the board. The countdown starts. He draws a thick vertical line.

"It's a line! *In the Line of Fire!*"

He shakes his head.

"It's a stick! Slapstick comedy! The Three Stooges!"

He keeps shaking his head.

"It's a pole! *Striptease*! It's a big stick—big penis—is it a porno?"

He laughs and draws another stick and then draws a circle around the bottom of both of them and then what looks like a mountain around it and then he draws a stick figure holding onto the sticks and then what are clearly skis on its feet.

"Oh he's skiing! It's a ski movie!"

Chase points to her to keep going and points at the skis.

"Skis! Oh oh oh! *The Big Lebowski!*"

"Yes!" Chase yells out as he grabs another card from the box and looks at it while he erases the board. He draws a simple face with a squiggly line on its forehead."

"Harry Potter! *Scarface!*"

"Yes!"

"Time!"

They hug, and we all clap for them, but secretly we hate them because come on—*Scarface* is easy.

Aimee's up, and she draws a big circle.

"It's a ball," Chase says, leaning forward in his chair.

"Yes!" she squeals.

"A basketball. *Hoop Dreams. Teen Wolf.*"

She shakes her head and continues to draw a bunch of squares on the ball.

"It's a golf ball. *Caddyshack.*"

She draws little lines that are radiating off of the ball and then one line attached to the top of the ball.

"It's a ceiling lamp. *National Lampoon's Vacation.*"

Then she draws a crescent shape.

"It's a moon. *Apollo 13. Man on the Moon. First Man.*"

She shakes her head vehemently and then draws a big nose with something in its nostril.

"A nose—is that a booger? *Boogie Nights!*"

They almost get another point for *Home Alone*, but time runs out and Chase is getting laid tonight no matter what, so what does he care. I slow clap for him.

"Well done, you two! Three points!" the manager says. "Up next we have Keaton and Roxy! Well, well, well!"

I do not like the way this guy is eyeing my fake girlfriend.

"You want to draw first?" I ask her.

"Damn right I do," she says. "Don't blow it." She erases the board and carefully picks out an index card, stares at it, frowns at me, puts the card facedown on the table, and then nods at the manager to start the timer. She draws what is obviously some kind of bird.

"It's a bird," I say.

She signals for me to keep going.

"It's a swan. *Black Swan.*"

She shakes her head and finishes drawing the bird.

"It's a duck. *Mighty Ducks. One Flew Over the Cuckoo's Nest.*"

She scowls at me.

"*Angry Birds.*"

She draws an arrow through the bird and blood spilling out of it.

"Whoa. It's a dead bird. *To Kill a Mockingbird!*"

"Yes!"

She grabs another card and erases the board, and I start pumping my fist like an idiot. "Yeah, babe!"

She furrows her brow at me while she rapidly draws a stick figure in a dress, sitting on a chair, with its legs spread out, and then she draws what looks like a vertical mouth in between the woman's legs.

"*Basic Instinct.*"

"Yes!"

We still have time for one more—she grabs a card, frantically erases the board, and then draws two circles, colors in one of them, and then draws what is obviously a pill bottle and then a question mark over the circles.

"They're pills, two pills—*The Matrix!*"

"Time!"

"*How the hell?*" Bernie shouts out.

"Do you choose the red pill or the blue pill?" I say. *Obviously.*

I get up to grab Roxy and kiss her, fast and hard, on the mouth, and she doesn't even resist it because we are the best couple here and everyone else can suck it.

"Wooo!" she claps her hands. "Come on, baby, three more points! Let's go for three more! We got this!"

"Easy," I say, winking at her. I erase the board and then pick out an index card. I grin at her, because we have so got this, and we are made for each other, and I am so getting laid tonight. I signal to the manager to start the timer, and I draw a perfect box.

"It's a box!" she yells out.

I nod and keep drawing.

"It's a boxing movie. *Rocky!*"

I shake my head.

"*The Fighter. Million Dollar Baby. Raging Bull. Ali. Southpaw.* That one with Denzel Washington, shit, *The Hurricane! Rocky Two! Rocky Three! Rocky Four!*"

I keep shaking my head, and then I finish drawing a head. In the box. And I keep pointing to it.

"Oh, there's something in the box. It's a gift. *The Gift.* It's a present. *Clear and Present Danger!*"

I look at her like she's crazy and shake my head.

"Draw something else! Hurry!"

I start drawing a book.

"It's a book. *The Jungle Book.* It's based on a book. Harry Potter!"

I draw a gun.

"A gun? *Top Gun?* Is it a James Bond movie?"

"*What?*"

"Time!"

Roxy slaps her forehead with both hands. "Oh my God!"

"It's *Seven.* That's a head in a box. It's the climax of the movie *Seven.* Literally anyone who has seen the movie would know that."

She stands up and places her fists on her hips because it wouldn't be enough of a statement to do that while she's sitting down. "*Seven? Seven?* Why didn't you just do seven lines so I could count out seven?"

"Because that would be too easy."

"It is literally your job to make it easy for me! I'm on your team!"

I am obstinate. We glare at each other. "Head in a box. Brad Pitt holding a gun. Iconic images."

"What was with the book?"

"It's the Bible. Seven deadly sins."

Roxy stares at my neck, and I honestly think she's trying to decide what kind of sharp object she should use to decapitate me with.

Everyone claps for us, but it's sad clapping. They feel bad for us. Because they know I'm not getting laid tonight or possibly ever again in my life.

"Mosquito food," she whispers to me.

"It's an iconic scene," I say because I never go down without a fight.

"Seven lines, and we would have been on to the next one."

"You and I both know you like a challenge, babe."

"Something you may not know about me—I like to win, *babe*," she says through gritted teeth.

I hold my hand up for her to slap it. "But good work on naming all those boxing movies. Proud of you, babe."

She doesn't slap my hand, but she does slap me on the shoulder. I don't cry out in pain too loudly, but it does startle the other guests.

"I will just pay for a massage, if that's what you want," I say to her, but she's already walking away from me to sit next to Aimee and Chase.

Chase winks at me and gives me the thumbs-up. "Well played," he says.

"Head in a box," I mutter stubbornly, crossing my arms in front of my chest as I sit down on a big comfortable sofa all by myself.

Maybe I can sleep here tonight.

CHAPTER 12
ROXY

Aimee pulls me aside as we're walking, as a group, from the lobby cottage up the long winding path to the guest cottages. "You have no idea how long I've been waiting to say this to you, Rox, but…" she says in a hushed voice, "you've got Wet Panty Face, my friend."

I stop walking so we can hang back. "What? No I don't. I have angry face. This is just me being angry."

"Are you sure you aren't angry because Keaton's penis isn't inside you?"

"Are you sure you aren't high?" Weak. That was a weak comeback. I'm off my game. But it's not because I have wet panty face. I know how to control my face. And my panties.

We walk very slowly and talk so quietly. "Just answer this one question."

"No."

"Are you attracted to…?" She points at Keaton's back with both index fingers.

I don't answer. I just I grab her hands to keep her from pointing and widen my eyes at her because *oh my God*. They're about thirty feet ahead of us, but geez.

"Because if you are, I totally get it. And I support it. Chase would lose his shit, but he doesn't need to know."

"Okay, I'm going to tell you something, but you cannot tell anyone, including Chase, and you cannot tell Keaton I told you." We stop walking again.

"Oh my God!" She raises her fists in the air. "You've already slept with him, haven't you?"

"No!" I grab her hands and pull them down to her sides. It's like trying to control a toddler.

"Really? Swear to Beyoncé?"

"Swear to all of Destiny's Child."

She accepts my no as the gospel truth.

"However..." I lower my voice, so low that I don't even know if she can hear me. "We made out at your wedding."

Her eyes go wide. "Wait, what? Say that again so I know for sure what you said."

I repeat, "We made out at your wedding."

She gasps. "You mean five years ago?!"

"Did you have another wedding that I don't know about?"

"I knew it!"

"You did not."

"I had no idea! I don't even believe you right now."

"It's true. It happened."

"Was it bad? Oh no—is he a bad kisser?"

"No." I look up the path, where he's walking with Chase and Matt and Bernadette. There is nothing cocky about the way he's walking right now—serves him right for not drawing seven little lines—but his butt is so cute in those jeans. "He's a good kisser. He's a really, really good kisser."

"Oh my God. Rox. You like him."

I scrunch up my face. "This is such a dumb conversation. I have mixed feelings about him. Do not tell him we talked about this."

"Of course I won't. Awww. Rox. This is so cute! And completely, totally unexpected and weird. It's really just very weird."

"Trust me, I know."

"But you didn't sleep with him that night?"

"No."

"Or at all since then?"

"No."

"Did you guys talk about it at all?"

"Not exactly."

"Ohhhh. That's why you kept trying to avoid him."

"Also because he drives me nuts."

"In your panties!"

"Yeah." I roll my eyes at her. "He drives my panties nuts." I cover my face. "Shit. He does. You're right. Keaton fucking Bridges is driving me nuts in my panties. And possibly in other parts of me that have absolutely no business even considering him. What is happening to me?"

"I don't know! Oh Rox, I wish I knew what to tell you! You used to give me such good advice when I was single—sometimes."

"Thank you for remembering."

"But I honestly don't know what to tell you."

Keaton and Chase stop to look back at us. We immediately start pointing at things, like we're having an in-depth discussion about the local flora back here. We wave them on, signal for them not to wait for us.

"Because it's crazy," I say to her. "Right?"

"It's not crazy. I mean, in a way, it makes total sense. If you guys were really a couple, I mean..." Even in the moonlight I can tell she's tearing up. "I mean, how perfect would that be? We'd all be coupled-up. Finn's godparents would be a real couple."

"But..."

"But if you guys fool around and it doesn't work out..."

"Yeah. And it wouldn't work out. I mean, how could it work out?"

"Well...you don't know. You might be good at being a girlfriend with him."

"Whoa." I stop in my tracks and squeeze her arm.

"I didn't mean—"

"You think *I'm* the one who would be the problem? Not 'head in the box'?"

"It's just that you—"

"Haven't been in a relationship for years."

"It's not like I think you—"

"Good. Because it's not that I'm incapable of being in a relationship anymore, and it's not that I don't want to be in a relationship again—I want to be in a relationship. I want it. I just haven't met the right guy for me at this point in my life. I don't think..."

Aimee and I stare at each other for a few seconds,

because this is the first time that I have ever said this out loud. This is the first time I have ever said anything even remotely like this out loud, and I can tell she is trying so hard not to dance around. She takes my hand in hers and squeezes it, and we keep walking. "Well, Rox...I'm very happy to hear that you want to be in a relationship. But what do you think the right guy for you would be like at this point in your life?"

I pull my hand away. "Okay, we're done talking about this. Go make another baby with your husband who fell in love with you as soon as he saw you walk into a bar."

She raises her hands in the air and does a little jig. "Okay, but we will talk about this again, and we did talk about it just now, and I am so proud of you, Rox!"

"All right, just get out of my face."

"Okay, but I've decided you should definitely have sex with him!"

"Shhh! Keep your voice down."

"You can do this! You're Foxy Roxy. You can make anything work."

"Yeah. You're right."

"Get your tits out, baby! It's your vacation!" She covers her mouth and laughs at herself.

Good God. She's going to throw every obnoxious thing I ever said to her when she was single back at me.

"Get it, guuuuurl!" she whispers as she walks backwards to join her husband.

Okay, okay.

I'll get it.

I fluff up my hair and look down at my blouse and unbutton a button or two. I'm still wearing my black bikini. Thinking about the way he unhooked my bikini top has been sending delicious infuriating shivers through me all day. I adjust the elastic waistband of my skirt.

Yeah.

I'm gonna go get me some of that Best Man now.

I will reach deep down inside to access my inner Foxy Roxy—circa ten years ago. The one who knows how to live in the moment. The one who knows that sex can just be a fun and satisfying thing that a man and a woman enjoy together simply because they're both single and attracted to each other. The one who knows that sex with Keaton Bridges will be hot despite the fact that I want to dropkick him—or because of it.

Okay.

The tits are out.

I'm gonna Rox his socks off—oh wait, he isn't wearing any.

When I get to the Hibiscus Cottage, Keaton has unlocked the front door and he's casually leaning against it, holding it open. His eyes lock on mine as I pass through the doorway. I step inside and wait for him to shut the door. I reach out to grab on to his shirt, but while I'm doing that, he takes a step towards me, backing me up against the wall. I now have Surprised Wet Panty Face. He cups my face with one hand and grabs my ass cheek with the other, and he stares down at me in our moonlit room with his eyes half-closed, nostrils flaring, lips hovering an inch above mine, and *holy shit what is happening?*

That moment.

We're back to that moment at the wedding. When he asked me with a look—*Should we?* Except this time, he's telling me with his look: *We should.* But he's still hovering, waiting for me to answer.

I nod, so quickly, just barely, as I stare at his mouth.

His thumb brushes my lower lip, and then he kisses me, with a low rumble from the back of his throat and five years' worth of pent-up heat and frustration and just the right amount of tongue.

I fumble with the buttons of his shirt, but he stops kissing me for one second to pull his shirt over his head and toss it away. My hands frantically explore his chest and arms and back, like they know they have to experience as much of him as possible before my brain catches up and tells them to knock it off. He tugs at my hair to pull my head back and expose my neck, and goddammit he goes straight for that spot right below my ear, the one that makes my knees go weak again as soon as his lips press against it.

This time, I just let the wall prop me up and let him continue to make me weak all over.

He strokes the nape of my neck lightly with his fingers while kissing up one side of my neck and then along my jaw to my mouth, where he kisses me, light and fleeting like a butterfly, and then slides his tongue in to penetrate and explore. He massages my hips and then my ass, and he's kissing me so deeply, like he means it, like he needs it—*oh dear God this man can kiss.*

Everything inside me is dropping and lurching and flipping and soaring to such great heights and waiting impatiently to fall again.

His hands find my breasts, cupping and massaging them, and that low rumble becomes a moan.

His hands. They may be manicured, but they can be rough. And I love it.

He's so hungry for me, and for just this moment it makes me want to give him everything I have to give.

I don't care if it's because he hasn't been with a woman for a while or if it's because this is me.

I don't even care that this is Keaton Bridges.

Or that I may just be having some insane reaction to him because I haven't been with anyone like this for a year.

I reach down to palm the hard-as-rock bulge in the front of his jeans.

"Fucking hell," he exhales.

Fucking hell is right.

This is going to be quick and dirty, and then we will never speak of it again.

"You need to get inside me immediately."

"Darlin'," he says, as he begins to unbutton my blouse, "I respectfully disagree."

He continues to carefully unbutton every button, so slowly it is agonizing, and then he pushes it down over my shoulders and kisses the bare skin on my right shoulder and slowly peppers kisses just below my collarbone all the way across to my left shoulder, pushing the sleeves down until I lift my hands out of them.

My hands go straight to his face for some reason, and I start kissing him like a crazy teenager. I don't know what's happening to me. I just really have to kiss him. He waits for me to calm the fuck down, and when I do, I lean back against the wall again, my hands tucked behind my tailbone.

He drags his fingertips down my chest, slowly, lightly, from my clavicle down to my cleavage, and then reaches behind my back to unhook my bikini top and swiftly reaches up behind my neck to untie the straps and lets it fall to the floor.

He stares at me. His jaw goes slack and his eyelashes flutter for a second, and then he regains control of himself. "Roxy fucking Carter," he says, his voice so low and deep. "Goddamn."

He takes one step to the side, slides one arm behind my shoulders and one behind my knees, and lifts me up to carry me to the bed. As soon as my back is on the mattress, his lips begin their delicious downhill journey. From my lips to my neck to my breasts to my belly and down, down, down.

"Fucking hell," I whisper. I force my eyelids open and raise my head to see where he went.

He's kneeling on the floor, looks up at me while reaching under my skirt and slowly pulling my bikini bottom down. He swiftly pushes my skirt up to my waist and hikes one of my legs over his shoulder. He massages my hips again—God, why does that feel so good—and then turns his head to kiss and nibble on my inner thigh, slowly, slowly moving closer to the part of me that is dying for him. When he's close enough that he could kiss me there, he teases my clit with his warm breath and the tip of his tongue, and—dammit—the anticipation has me trembling.

"Goddammit, Keaton," I whisper. I run my hands

through his hair while his tongue circles and flicks and sweeps. The long, slow licks have me shuddering. The way he continues to stroke my hips and my ass and my thighs, my whole body feels attended to and worshipped. The way he's moaning and humming while he performs tongue gymnastics, it creates vibrations that I feel everywhere. My hips move in rhythm with his tongue as it probes in and out, and then two fingers slide in and out and twist and curl, and just as I start to tense up, his fingers pull out and he sucks hard on my clit.

"Oh shit!" I cry out. I grab on to his shoulders near his neck and squeeze tight. He digs his fingernails into my ass and groans, and that's when I remember the sunburn. "Oh shit! Sorry! Did I hurt you?"

"Nothing hurts right now," he mutters, and then he goes back to sucking and stimulating my G spot until I've come so hard, I'm surprised I haven't crushed his face and fingers.

Okay. Now let's get this next part over with before it turns into a whole big thing.

He stands up and reaches into the pocket of his jeans, producing a condom package, and tears the wrapper with his teeth. *Fucker.* Has he been planning for this all night?

He steps out of his jeans, pulls down his boxers, palms his *very erect whole big thing oh my God Keaton what the fuck,* and then rolls the condom on. He climbs on top of me and positions himself, kissing me deeply while slowly pressing inside me and moaning. Jesus, he fills me up, but I'm so wet, my body's just like *yeah, get him in here.*

My hips start rocking immediately, and my legs wrap

around his waist. He groans once and thrusts slowly at first and then picks up the pace, and eventually he is drilling me and it feels so good and I'm on the brink of orgasm again and I clench around him and think *this is it, here we go, he's gonna come now.*

But he doesn't.

He drags me with him to the edge of the bed. I open my eyes and find him standing there. He lifts my bent legs up to rest my feet flat against his chest, slides his hands down to raise up my hips, and then he's penetrating me from an amazing angle, and it's like he's launched a bottle rocket inside me that explodes in my brain. The quakes hit my entire body, and the aftershocks keep coming until I realize he's still thrusting away and panting.

Surely he's going to come now.

But he doesn't.

He maneuvers me over to the corner of the bed, flips me over, and spreads my legs on either side of the corner of the mattress, and then he holds on to my hips and pulls me to him with each thrust.

Jesus Christ, it's like when he kept tricking me into telling him about my family at dinner last night, but this time he's tricking me into having orgasms.

Keaton fucking Bridges!

This time it's the awareness of him and the sounds he's making as he allows himself to get closer to the brink that make me come again. The way he's grunting as he slams into me and says my name over and over, his deep voice getting higher and higher, and then finally he gets so tense and quiet, and there's the slow emptying of his lungs and the heat of him emptying himself inside me, and the way he holds me so tight while he shakes and his voice goes deep again. I slowly lower myself to the mattress so I can feel the weight of him on my back.

We're both covered in sweat, and it's beautiful.

He worked so hard, and it was beautiful.

He lazily kisses the top of my shoulder, and it's beautiful.

Our breaths are still fast and heavy and in sync, and it's beautiful.

His hands find mine and he laces our fingers together, and it's beautiful.

So much for quick and dirty.

When he finally slides off me and retreats to the bathroom, the skin on my back feels cold.

I crawl up to the head of the bed, remove the skirt that still somehow remains around my waist, and get under the covers.

Seriously—what just happened?

Goddammit, I want to do that again.

And that's exactly why I can't.

I guess I was fooling myself to think that I could just bone Keaton Bridges and not have it mean something.

It means something.

He may not be my friend exactly, but he's in my circle of best friends, and he matters.

I may have had a lot of sex in my life, and what we just did may have been fun and amazing, and okay, it blew my mind, but this feels like something that could get real and serious—fast.

When I fall, I fall hard, and I'm afraid I'm too old to fall for someone it's not going to work out with.

And it can't possibly work out for Keaton and me.

I mean, it can't possibly.

Right?

When he returns and gets into bed, he caresses my arm. I look over and smile at him—the sultry, warm, and appreciative smile that he deserves, except the words that come out are all wrong. I say, "That was amazing. Really amazing... I'm gonna sleep on my side. So I don't snore and keep you awake."

He pulls his hand away. "Great. Thanks. I agree, that was amazing."

I turn over. When my back is to him, I whisper a friendly, "Good night!"

"Good night, Roxy Carter," he grumbles.

I can hear him laugh quietly and scrub his face with his hands.

I know, Keaton. I know.

I'm the worst.

"I mean, you were really, *really* amazing," I say. "Good job."

Oh God, stop talking, Roxy, I'm begging you.

"Thanks, I really appreciate the feedback."

"Okay, cool. Good night. Again. Keaton."

"Good night again, Roxy Carter."

I love how he says my name.

I'm screwed.

CHAPTER 13
KEATON

I wake up alone in bed, with two words on my mind: Roxy and *saudade*.

Roxy is a word that used to mean "Aimee's best friend," and "hot" and "obnoxious," and then five years ago it just became a word that had a question mark after it, but now all of a sudden, it means so many things to me I can't even count them.

Saudade is a Portuguese word, one that has no English equivalent and is nearly impossible to translate. You just know it when you feel it. It was the first untranslatable word that my hot linguistics professor taught us, and it's the one that intrigued me the most. The simplest way to describe it is "a melancholy or longing for someone or something that's absent." But it's so much more than that. It brings happy and sad feelings. There's wistfulness and hope there. It's an emptiness that you believe can only be filled by the thing you feel *saudade* for—whether it's something you've experienced before or something you dream of—but there's a pleasant suffering in knowing that this thing is somehow out of reach.

It's what Roxy and I were both feeling that night of Chase and Aimee's wedding, although we never spoke of it. That yearning for the way things were back when we were all hanging out together all the time. That yearning for the thing that Chase and Aimee had found in one another.

That thing for me now is Roxy.

It's her body and everything I saw and felt and heard last night and what I didn't get to see and do or say.

It's who she is deep down when she isn't being the Roxy Carter she presents to the world.

It's those moments when I sense that she gets me in ways that most people never will and those moments when I'm dying for her to want to know more.

It isn't love yet, I know that, but I know what the potential for love feels like, and this is it. She's the last woman I ever would have predicted I'd feel this for when I met her. But by now I know what it takes to keep me interested in someone, and she has what it takes to be the last woman I ever want to feel this for.

When I was in my teens and twenties, I loved the chase, but once I'd captured a girl's heart or some other part of her, all I could think about were all the other doors that would be closing if I was with this one person for the rest of my life. But with Roxy, I just know that there will always be more doors to open and they're all hers. I know it. In my heart and in my soul.

And yeah, okay, I also feel it in my balls, and I don't

know if I can go on living if I can't have sex with her again, repeatedly, in every way possible.

Last night was great. It was great for me and I know it was great for her, but she was holding back. Maybe it was because I caught her off guard, or maybe it was because she wanted it to be a one-time thing. It was just like after we kissed five years ago, only she couldn't walk away this time, so she just went to sleep.

I'm not saying I have a profound sense of bittersweet homesickness for Roxy's pussy, but I'm not *not* saying it either.

There's still so much I want from her.

I still haven't seen her fully naked in broad daylight.

I still haven't felt her mouth on my cock.

I still haven't made her scream my name while she's coming.

I'm staring up at the ceiling through the mosquito net, and I can hear her hushed, husky voice out on the veranda. It sounds like she's talking to her assistant. It's Sunday, I think, but they're catching up on things from Friday and discussing the coming week. From what I gather, it sounds like there's someone at work who's competitive with her and trying to make some moves while she's on vacation. I could help her with that. I could help her with anything if she'd let me. She's friendly with her assistant in a way that I never have been with mine. She's friendly with her assistant in a way that she never has been with me.

I hike myself up on my elbows. I don't even know what time it is. I slept straight through the night. She didn't snore at all, or if she did it didn't wake me. It looks like she's already showered and fully dressed. It looks like she is in no way feeling *saudade* or anything else for me or what we did last night, and it hurts just a little.

I'm going to have to play this right. I'm going to have to take it slow. I'm going to have to negotiate with her in such a way that she doesn't realize we're negotiating a deal, and then I'm going to build something beautiful for us, from the ground up.

I reach for my phone on the bedside table and lie back down.

When she ends the call with her assistant, I slide down under the covers and initiate a call with Roxy.

After two rings, she answers, "Seriously?"

"I'm just calling as a courtesy to say that I thoroughly enjoyed spending time with you last night."

"Thank you, I also had a very nice time." I can hear her smiling. "I appreciate the call and I am hanging up now."

"My pleasure, and so am I."

She hangs up, and I do the same. When I re-emerge from under the covers, I find her walking toward my side of the bed. I can see an animal-print bikini under her lightweight white dress, and I can smell the cocoa butter sunscreen, and it does all kinds of things to every part of me.

She gives me a little wave. "Morning."

"What time is it?"

"About eight thirty."

I nod and sit up, rake my fingers through my hair. It does not go unnoticed, the way her eyes slowly lower from my hands to my forearms to my bare chest. When she notices me noticing, she looks down at the floor.

"Everything okay at work?"

"Yeah, fine. Under control."

"Is it?"

"Yeah."

"Because if there's anything you want to talk about..." I point to myself with my thumbs.

"Everything's fine at work," she says, pointedly crossing her arms in front of her chest. "Under control."

"Good. Cool." *We'll revisit that later.*

"So, last night was fun and everything, but...are we cool?"

"I mean, I'm cool. I don't know about you. Are you cool?"

She rolls her eyes and smirks at me. "I mean, we don't have to be weird about it and make a big deal, right? We had sex. That's it."

"We did have sex. And that is it." I stretch my arms overhead and watch as she stares at my flexing muscles.

"Good. Great."

"Fuckin' A." I scratch my pecs. They aren't itchy, but I like watching her watch me.

She clearly hates that she can't stop staring at me. Poor thing. *You just go ahead and struggle with yourself, Roxy Carter. I'll be here, ready when you are.* She looks around, bites her lower lip, crosses one leg in front of the other, scratches her arm. She looks like an awkward teenager all of a sudden, and I love it. "Okay," she says. "So I'm gonna go have breakfast and let you shower, because I have a feeling you'll be beating off in there, and I don't really want to be around when you do that."

Well, that was pretty much the opposite of what I was expecting her to say, but she is absolutely right. "Enjoy your breakfast."

"Did you want me to bring you back something, or do you want me to wait down there for you, or..."

Well well, what a girlfriend-y thing to ask, Miss Carter. "I think I'll go for a run before I eat, actually. If that's okay with you."

She looks surprised that I said that. I fucking love it when I surprise her. "It is okay with me. Of course." She places both hands on the back of her hips. Not the fists on the hips thing that I'm used to. This particular stance straightens her posture and pushes her tits out and makes me want to die a little. "I'll probably just hang out on the beach and at the pool for most of the day. If that's okay with you."

"Sounds good."

She nods. "Okay, then. I'm gonna go."

"Okay. See you around."

"Okay, then." She claps her hands together, loudly, and then makes a face like she wishes she hadn't done that. Then she salutes me, slides into her flip-flops, grabs her bag and heads outside. She shuts the front door quietly, glancing back at me as she does, and I can't stop smiling because I can tell—I have no doubt—that what she's really doing is leaving a door cracked open for me.

. . .

An hour later, after I've FaceTimed the doggy hotel to confirm that Jackpot is still doing well and is still totally indifferent as to my whereabouts, after I've gone for a run, I grab a quick breakfast at the breakfast bar and text Aimee to see if she can come join me for a minute to chat.

AIMEE: Just me?
ME: If you can manage to get away from your husband without him coming after me with either a blunt or sharp object.
AIMEE: Everything okay?
ME: Is it that weird for me to want to hang out with my best friend's wife for a brief amount of time?
AIMEE: Sort of?
ME: Just come get a cup of coffee or whatever.
AIMEE: On my way.

I wonder if she's talked to Roxy. I wonder if she knows about last night. When she shows up, she's looking at me like she's expecting me to be bleeding from the head or something.

"Are you okay?"

"Yes. Are you?"

"I'm totally weirded out. Hi. Good morning. What's up?"

"You getting coffee?"

"I think I've already had enough. What's going on?" I search her face for clues, but she seems genuinely oblivious as to why I would want to have a chat with her.

There's no cool way to lead into this, so I'm just gonna go for it. "I was just wondering about your friend's relationship history."

She blinks and then rubs her lips together and smacks them. She's trying so hard not to smile. "You mean, *your girlfriend's* relationship history?"

"Correct. Needless to say, your husband does not need to know that I'm asking about this."

"Needless to say, Roxy doesn't need to know either."

"Agreed. Go on."

Aimee taps her chin with the tip of her index finger. "Well...I met her in college, you know? At Ann Arbor."

"I do."

"She already had a boyfriend when I met her. From high school. Tad."

"Tad?" *Come on. Tad?*

"She really loved him. Like, a lot. In that first love kind of way. They were cute together. He was nice. I liked him."

I fight the urge to stab myself in the thigh with my fork. I don't know why, but I really didn't think she'd ever been in love before. "Uh-huh."

"They had been together in high school, and they were together for the first two years of college, and the plan was that he'd move to New York after we graduated too. But then he decided to do a semester abroad in Ireland, and he never came back."

"Oh."

"She was kind of devastated."

"Oh."

"And it changed her. She had about a six-month mourning period, and then she just sort of...became Foxy Roxy."

"Interesting. So, no serious boyfriends since then?"

"Well, you know, she moved to Brooklyn before I did, and she had a pretty serious boyfriend for almost a year, I think. Jake. I never met him, but she seemed really happy with him. It was serious enough that he went with her to visit her parents at Thanksgiving."

"Okay." I fight the urge to pick up this table and throw it across the room.

"But then Jake went on tour—he was in a band. Drummer, I think."

"Of course."

"And they decided that it would be best if they weren't exclusive while he was on tour, and then it just sort of, you know. Fizzled out."

"Okay. And since then?"

"Nothing serious. That's when she really embraced the whole *work hard/play hard* thing. Or she did, I mean. I don't think she's been playing very hard lately."

"Interesting. Why do you think that?"

Her mouth becomes one straight line. "Um. I probably shouldn't talk about this with you."

"Very interesting."

"I mean—with anyone. I shouldn't be talking about this with anyone."

"And can you confirm that you have had at least one conversation with her regarding yours truly?"

"I cannot and will not confirm nor deny it."

I fight the urge to jump up on the table and start rapping about what a badass motherfuckin' baller my dick is. "Uh-huh. And what are your thoughts on the matter of a hypothetical potential relationship between myself and Miss Roxy Carter?"

Aimee's face erupts into a giant smile, and she bounces around in her chair and then finally manages to control her facial muscles. She clears her throat. "Well, first of all, both my husband and I will kill you if you fuck around with her."

"Define fucking around with her."

"Wooing her and having sex with her and then losing interest and never seeing her again. Leading her to believe that you have feelings for her and then bolting when she actually returns those feelings for you. Being a dick to her in any way even for a minute."

Who is this asshole that my best friends have me confused with? I gulp down the last of my coffee. "Define 'I will kill you.'"

"I will be so mad at you and not want to see or speak to you for a really long time. Like a month, probably."

"Got it."

She looks me straight in the eye. "You haven't already...have you?"

She can look all she wants. A gentleman never tells—especially when he doesn't want to get castrated—and I've got my poker face on. "I'm sure she'd tell you if we had." I examine her reaction. She may have a poker face herself, this one.

"That's true." She shrugs. "Well, anyway." She stands up and puts her sunglasses back on. "I'm gonna head back to the pool. I think Roxy's sunning herself on the beach."

I nod. "Cool. I'm gonna go for a walk. I'll see you guys later."

"Yeah." She punches me on the bicep. "See you later."

I watch Aimee practically skip away, and I am about ninety percent sure that Roxy told her that we had sex last night and one hundred percent certain that I have Aimee's approval to pursue her. I just need to keep it from Chase until it's a real thing.

I hang out at the pool with Matt and Bernie for about half an hour because Aimee and Chase have already disappeared back to their cottage. We talk about going sailing tomorrow, until it becomes crystal clear to me that Matt and Bernie have no intention of exerting any energy while they're here except when they're in bed.

Good for them.

They excuse themselves because it's been like two hours since they last had sex with each other probably, so I decide to wander down to the beach to see what Roxy's up to.

I mentally prepare myself to find her sunning herself, tits-up in that leopard print bikini, but instead I find her still in that white dress, kneeling on the sand, not far from the high tide line. She has a look of determination on her face as she pounds the sand in front of her into submission.

"You building a sandcastle?"

"I got on Aimee's FaceTime with Finn, and he asked me to build a sandcastle and send him pictures. I got the buckets and shovels from the front desk and borrowed a knife and spoon from the breakfast bar." She sighs while continuing to pummel. "It's been a while since I've done this."

"You want some help?"

She places a plastic bucket at my feet. "I need more water. Where's everyone else?" she asks without looking up.

"Fucking in their cottages."

"Already?"

"I guess some people are into that sort of thing," I say as I kick off my flip-flops and stroll down to the water's edge. When I return with a full bucket, I tell her, "You need a water hole. Dig down until you find water so you have a supply. So you don't have to keep going to the sea for it."

She passes me a plastic shovel. "Sounds good."

I remove my shirt, drop to my knees beside her, and start digging with the shovel, and then I just use my hands. It does not go unnoticed that she keeps glancing over at my hands.

I survey the foundation she's built. "What is this? A one-bedroom?"

"It's going to be a box." She grins up at me. "You can help me with the head."

When I realize what she's making, my head falls back, and I laugh so hard. A head in a box. "Finn will love it."

"I know. I can't wait to watch *Seven* with him. How long do you think I should wait? Until he's...?" She makes seven slashes in the sand and arches an eyebrow at me.

"Hey. *I* will be the one introducing him to that bit of cinematic genius. When he's ten."

"I called dibs."

"I call bullshit. I don't believe you want to watch that with him. I say we both have a movie night with him. Together."

She gives me the side-eye. "Together? That doesn't sound very cool to me." Her voice is teasing but hesitant. "You aren't still thinking about last night, are you?"

"What about it? I'm definitely not thinking about the way you taste or the little noises you make when you're kissing me or the way you lose the ability to stand when I kiss you on your neck, right—" I put my hand on the back of her neck and rub that spot just below her ear with my thumb "—there."

She closes her eyes and sways the tiniest bit.

"And I have no intention of trying to persuade you to let me kiss you right now, just once, just for show, or just for the hell of it because kissing's fun and good and we're both really good at kissing each other."

She's staring at my mouth and her lips are moving, and I think she may be trying to say something but nothing's coming out.

"What's that now?"

She licks her lips. "Screw you, Bridges," she whispers

as she leans in and lets me kiss her. Soft and slow and deliberate, the way you carefully smooth out wet sand after pounding it down until there are no more weak spots, adding layer upon layer, pushing and smoothing, and then it finally begins to take the shape of something you could see yourself living in.

Or finding someone's head inside of.

I keep the kisses soft and slow and deliberate, even as her breath quickens and the little moans get louder, until she pulls away and stands up and says, "I'm going for a walk."

I clear my throat. "To cool off?"

"To let you cool off."

"Are you coming back?"

She raises her hand in the air, a vague gesture that could mean anything, but I know what it means.

You'll be back, Roxy Carter. You'll be back. And I'll be here, the king of my fucking castle waiting for you.

Or with a really awesome head in a box.

Whatever.

Whatever you're ready for today.

CHAPTER 14
ROXY

"You aren't going to know this," Matt states while staring at the slip of paper in his hand.

"Rude!" Bernadette yells out. "Try me!"

They're both standing front and center in the lobby, and the timer is counting down from one minute.

"Baseball Hall of Fame pitcher for the Mariners and the Diamondbacks. 'The Big Unit.'"

"Babe Ruth!"

"Pass."

Bernadette balls up her fists. "Rude!"

Matt returns that piece of paper to the basket and pulls another one from it. "That singer you and Tommy like that I can't stand."

"Christina Aguilera!"

"The other one."

"Katy Perry!"

"Other one."

"Taylor Swift!"

"Yes." He drops that slip of paper and draws another

one from the basket, glancing over at Don and Debbie, the oldest couple here. "He's in old movies with his brothers, and he has bushy eyebrows and a mustache and glasses and a cigar."

"Groucho Marx!"

Matt tosses the piece of paper aside and grabs another one. Don and Debbie look disappointed and surprised that Bernadette actually got that one, but they don't realize she has the soul of an eighty-year-old.

Matt almost laughs. "That model you think I look like, but I don't."

"David Gandy!"

"Time!" the resort manager calls out, as half the guests ask who David Gandy is and half of them insist that Matt is way better-looking. He kind of is.

"We got three!" Bernadette claps.

"Only two points, I'm afraid," the manager says. "You lose one point when you take a pass. Good job, though!"

Bernadette screws up her adorable face and grunts. "You should have kept going!" she says to her husband.

"Name one other celebrity pitcher besides Babe Ruth, who by the way, was more of an outfielder than a pitcher."

She punches his bicep and grunts again because she can't name anyone else. She still hates that he knows her so well, but it's sweet. Must be tough, having such a gorgeous husband who loves and understands and supports you.

"Up next are Mr. Chase and Mrs. Aimee McKay!" the manager calls out.

Keaton and I give each other a look. Mr. and Mrs. Perfect Couple—why do we always have to go after them? He rests his hand on top of mine—a bold move, considering I've barely said ten words to him since he tricked me into kissing him this morning. When I got back from my walk, we finished the sand head-in-a-box in silence. We wordlessly agreed to make it a zombie head, which was an obvious choice, since Finn likes zombies and we wouldn't want to have to explain to him whose head is in the box in the movie and ruin the surprise when he watches it.

The six of us all had dinner together at a restaurant in town, which was wonderful, and while I didn't say much directly to him, I've never been so aware of Keaton when we were in a group before. I keep thinking he needs to lighten up or loosen up, but he's actually a nice, funny guy, and maybe I just needed to loosen up when I'm around him. I might even like him. Every minute it gets less and less mystifying and terrifying. Some strange island magic is transforming my animosity toward him into straight-up lust and something that feels like...fondness?

I don't move my hand away, but I don't lace my fingers with his either.

We watch as Aimee pulls a piece of paper from the basket and the countdown timer starts. She and Chase are standing a few feet apart, but they lean in toward each other, and it just says so much.

"He's the rock star who goes best with mashed potatoes!" Aimee yells out while doing a little hop.

"Meat Loaf."

"Yes!" She drops the paper and grabs another one. "I like big butts and I cannot lie!" she raps.

"Kim Kardashian."

"Woohoo!" Keaton applauds and gets my elbow in his ribs.

"He's that golfer," Aimee says.

"Tiger Woods."

"He sculpted David."

"Michelangelo."

"Oh God—that bald guy from the street racing movies you like that I can't watch."

"Shit." Chase stares at the floor because he can't remember his name.

"Oh! His last name is not *gas*, it's..."

"Vin Diesel!"

"Yes!"

"Time!"

Chase and Aimee double-high-five each other, and the manager declares that they have tied the resort's record for most points in one round.

Keaton pulls me up from the sofa—I had forgotten that he was holding my hand. "You asking the questions this round?"

"Do you really have to ask?"

"Pick a good one, baby," he says as I reach for a piece of paper in the basket.

I'm pretty sure no one can tell that my stomach just did a little backflip when he called me baby. I stare down at the celebrity name. "He developed a theory of evolution."

"Darwin."

I drop that piece of paper like it's hot and swipe another one. "The pop artist who did the Campbells soup things."

"Warhol."

Two-for-two. "That gay, witty author and playwright."

"David Sedaris."

"London. Nineteenth Century."

"Oscar Wilde."

"Yes!" I try to control my smile as I look at him while picking the next one. He winks at me while rubbing his hands together. "Ummm…" I lower my voice, cue up my best Texas drawl, and look at him like an intense stoner. "All right, all right, all right!"

"Matthew McConaughey."

I pick another one. "Okay. He's a martial artist guy."

"Bruce Lee."

"The other one."

"Chow Yun-fat."

"Who?"

"Jet Li."

"Keep going."

"Sammo Hong…Donnie Yen."

"The only one I would know besides Bruce Lee."

"Jackie Chan!"

"Yes!"

"Time!"

"Oh my God," I say, shaking my fists at him like an angry old lady. "You're supposed to think like me! That's kind of the point of this."

"Calm down, baby," he says, rubbing my back. "We won."

"*We did?*"

"Well not yet, but we tied Chase and Aimee. That's sort of like winning."

"Five points for Mr. Keaton and Miss Roxy!" the manager declares.

"Oh my God!" I say, smiling at him like an idiot, and then I *don't* kiss him, and it feels like the most unnatural thing in the world.

I look over at Chase and Aimee. Aimee is beaming, and Chase's eyebrows are furrowed. "Tied!" I say to them. "We're tied." I look over at Matt and Bernadette. "We beat you. No bigs. Just sayin'."

"I put Warhol in there, by the way," says Bernadette. "So I kind of helped you. Just sayin'."

When Keaton and I sit back down on the sofa, we're sitting closer to each other than we were before. He stretches and puts his arm around me. Don and Debbie are eyeing us because they're up next.

"So," I whisper to Keaton. "You some kind of kung fu movie nerd?"

"Big-time. I can't wait to watch them with Finn."

"Yeah? Well, what if I want to watch them too?"

He grins. "I will send you a list of my favorites."

I nudge his arm with my elbow.

"And I will watch them with you and Finn anytime."

"I mean..." I lean in to whisper in his ear. "I never said we can't be friends."

He turns to whisper in my ear. "I never thought we weren't friends."

· · ·

Don and Debbie end up kicking all of our asses, but really, they need the couples massages more than we do. They've been together forty-five years.

When we're about to head back to the cottages, Aimee and Bernadette tell the guys to go ahead, and then they drag me into the ladies' room. They have this intense expression on their faces but like they're trying to seem all easy-going. I feel cornered and trapped, and I have a feeling they're either about to try to sell me Tupperware or vitamin supplements or they're going to try to convince me to join a cult. "What is happening?"

"You guys are so cute together it's not even funny," Aimee says.

Ah. They're going to try to sell me on joining their married-person cult.

"You know, Matt and I were very different too when we first met," Bernadette tells me, as if this is a shocking revelation.

I give Aimee a look.

"I didn't tell her—she guessed and asked me, and I couldn't lie to her!"

"Okay, first of all," I say to Bernadette, "you and Matt are still very different, and secondly, Keaton is not Matt."

"But Keaton's amazing. He's so cute with Harriet."

"He's so great with Finn."

"*I'm* great with Harriet and Finn!"

Bernadette's head jerks back. "Nobody said you weren't."

"See, that's your problem right there," Aimee says.

"You're competitive with him. You don't have to be competitive with him. It's not like there's only ever been room for one single friend in this group."

"Okay, that is not true. What about the times when Chase couldn't make it to a work event and you could only pick one plus-one, and sometimes you'd choose Keaton instead of me?" I don't even care about this stuff so much right now. It just feels like I need to keep acting the way they expect me to. That's the thing about being a part of a group. It's not easy to change how people see you.

Aimee waves her hand dismissively. "That only happened when Keaton knew people at the event and it made sense for him to go instead of you. And anyway, if you're still mad at him for being such an ass to Chase and me when we first got together, I appreciate how loyal you are, but you need to get over it. Chase and I did. I love Keaton."

"I loooove Keats," Bernadette says with her hands over her heart.

"Really? That much?"

"One day last year, we needed a backup babysitter really fast, and he literally dropped everything to come look after Harriet."

"Why didn't you ask me to babysit?"

"We did. You had a dinner thing that you couldn't get out of. Anyway—when we came home, she was fast asleep, and he was covered in glitter and face paint, and he was wearing a construction paper crown that she'd made him and she made him promise he wouldn't take it off even when she was asleep."

"What did she paint on his face?" Aimee asks, thank God, because I'm dying to know.

"A butterfly. He let her paint a pink and blue butterfly on his face. We took a picture of him like that, and she has it up in her room—oooh, it's on my phone. I'll show you! And before you ask, Roxy—yes, she also has a picture of you from that time we had a picnic." Bernadette starts to frantically scroll through images on her phone.

"Thank you, but I do not need to see the picture."

"Well, I want to see it," Aimee says.

"You know what you should do?" Bernadette says, waving her phone at me. "You should try *converge-sating* with him."

"I don't know what that is, but I'm not doing that. Okay, I'm gonna go."

"We don't want to scare her," Aimee says to Bernadette. "We aren't pressuring you, girl. Just chill."

"I'm chill. I just...this isn't the kind of thing I can rush into. All right? This could be...a big deal."

"The biggest!" Aimee raises her hands in the air again.

"Okay, I'm leaving."

"But no pressure."

"But wait!" Bernadette grabs my arm. "What you just said—that's the thing. You've been resisting Keaton and holding on to this idea of him being an ass for so long because deep down, you *know* how life-changing it would be to give in to all that energy between you. There's so much of it, Roxy, I could paint it. In fact, I probably will. My next series of paintings just might be about you and Keaton."

"I think that might count as pressure," Aimee stage whispers to her.

I can't even process what she just said. "Okay, good night!"

"*Roxton foreva!*" Bernadette calls out as I'm opening the door to the hallway.

"Shhh!" I shut the door again. "Let me get my head around *Roxton for now* first. I mean, I don't even know where he's at yet."

I look at Aimee, who is smiling down at the floor and trying to hide her face with her hair like a lunatic. "Also, to be clear," she says to Bernadette, "Chase can't know. I mean, not until they're officially, you know. Together. Because we don't even know if Keaton's really interested." She smacks her lips together and looks to the side.

I get up in her sweet face until she has to look me in the eyes. "Did he talk to you or something?"

She covers her mouth. "Did who talk to me?"

"Girl. Do not make me slap you."

CHAPTER 15
KEATON

By the time Roxy gets back to the Hibiscus Cottage, I'm already in bed, shirtless and looking at photos of Jackpot on my phone. He played outside in the snow today. Most likely took a dump for the good people of the doggy hotel in the snow too. Good for him. He's probably enjoying my vacation more than I am. I know for sure that he's going to enjoy the rest of this night more than I will.

I made a decision earlier tonight, that I will wait for Roxy to make the next move. No matter how long I have to wait, no matter how painful it will be to stay on my side of the bed. I'll let her think that I'm not capable of thinking like her, but I know this is what she needs. My M.O. in the past has been to come on strong with the women I want, but this woman is more strong-willed than most. I have definitely met my match, and I just need to be patient and wait for her to realize that she's met hers.

It has probably only been fifteen minutes since I got here, but it feels like I've been waiting for her to return from the lobby forever. There's an Inuit word —*iktsuarpok*. It's that anticipation and frustration you feel when you're waiting for someone to come over and you keep going outside to check for them. That's how I've been feeling for the past fifteen minutes. That's how I'm feeling all the time now, when it comes to Roxy Carter. I'm just waiting for her to show up for me, and I know that she will be worth the wait.

She shuts the door so quietly, as if she expects me to be asleep and doesn't want to wake me. She kicks off her sandals and tiptoes around, even when she sees that I'm sitting up. She doesn't make eye contact with me when she pulls a T-shirt out from her suitcase and then makes her way over to the bathroom.

Oh for fuck's sake—now what?

I turn off the bedside lamp, punch the pillow, and slam my head down into it, turning my back to the bathroom door. This woman confounds me and I love-hate it. I try to will myself to fall asleep before she gets into bed, which is impossible. I'm too aware of the sound of her moving behind the door. She isn't slamming anything— she isn't mad. She's carefully placing each of her many products back on the marble counter instead of tossing things around—she's being considerate. She's changing her behavior for me, or at least because of me. She's probably taking her birth control pill, which I just happened to see in her cosmetics bag. She's also taking her sweet fucking time in there, so she's either dreading getting into bed with me or she's figuring out a game plan.

Or maybe she's doing that ten-step Korean skincare thing that Tamara tried for about a week.

Tamara.

I wish I hadn't thought of her. Now all of a sudden, this bed feels bigger and emptier and the distance between me and all of the women of the world feels greater. I've managed to stay so focused on the potential start of a relationship with Roxy all day, and now the prospect of going through another ending with someone —someone as significant as Roxy—almost paralyzes me.

Maybe I should just go outside and sleep in the fucking bathtub. Offer myself up to the mosquitos and the cruel gods of heartache and blue balls. I barely even feel the mattress move when she finally gets under the covers. I'm either numb, or I'm feeling so much that I can't feel any more.

She doesn't turn on the bedside lamp. She barely moves. "Good night," she says. A statement.

"Good night," I say. A resolution.

And that's it. We're down for the count. That's the end of our third night in bed together. We scored ten points in two rounds of Celebrity, and that's all the scoring I'll be doing tonight.

I'm in that hazy and bewildering world between being asleep and awake when I feel something on the back of my shoulders and realize—or hope—that they are lips and that Roxy is kissing me. If I'm dreaming, I don't want to wake up, and if I'm awake, I don't want to move because maybe she's asleep. She presses up against my back, and Sweet Jesus, she is naked. Her nipples brush against my bare skin as she strokes down my arm, reaches around and slides her hand down past the elastic waistband of my boxers, and caresses and tickles my balls. She pushes my boxers down, takes my cock in that hand, and *fucking hell* she knows how to handle me just right, but I am going to resist every urge to ramp things up, because I want to stay in this hazy and bewildering world for as long as possible.

Last night she ended up being so receptive, but tonight she's curious and exploring my body—either that or she's planning to take her time and drive me crazy—whatever her intentions, every part of me is along for the ride. She circles her index finger and thumb around me and takes her time stroking up and down my shaft and then uses her whole hand to do the same, coming up and palming the head and gently twisting and carefully rubbing and somehow knowing exactly when to drag her fingertips down to my balls again when the head gets too sensitive to take any more.

She nudges my arm to get me to shift onto my back so she can kneel between my legs. She's still under the covers, and all I hear is barely controlled heavy breathing and my own heartbeat and the movement of skin against bed sheets. I can't see much of anything, but I can feel everything. I reach out to pull her down for a kiss. She leans forward to sweep her nipples across my chest and then pulls away before my mouth can make contact with hers. She takes hold of my cock at the base with one hand, pressing her palm along the shaft and slowly pulling it toward her. When she reaches the tip, she does the same with her other hand, over and over, slowly and gently, and then she grips me harder, tugs up and down and goes back to gentle caresses.

Yeah. She's trying to drive me crazy, and I'm fine with it. I grab on to the sides of the pillow. My eyes are squeezed shut, my teeth clenched tight, and the veins in my neck might burst, but I am just fine with this.

When I feel her fingers at that spot behind my balls and her tongue licking up my rock-hard shaft, I finally break the silence with a groan and "Fucking hell, Roxy," and that's when I feel her climbing on top of me. Her bent knees are on either side of my hips, and she's lining up the crown of my throbbing cock with her hot, wet pussy. Torturing me. I take the deepest breath I'm capable of and wait for her to steadily lower herself down and put me out of my sweet misery. The meaning of life can now be measured in millimeters and warm, slippery inches, and I have never wanted so badly to feel connected to a woman.

I hold on to her hips, and when she finally sinks all the way down and she is filled up with me, her breath catches and she lets out a loud, sexy gasp, and I'm on fire. I squeeze her fleshy ass and wait for her to start rocking her hips, and when she does, it's a jolt to my system, and I can't hold back much longer.

Fuck it.

I sit up, and she arches her back, and my mouth is finally on those beautiful tits and my hands are everywhere, and I am starving and feasting and delirious for this woman's body. I almost make her come from all the licking and sucking. Her legs are wrapped around my waist and my legs are crossed under her and we are rocking back and forth together, and I am so glad I stretched after running today. I had no idea my body could do this, but right now I think I would do anything for her.

She finally kisses me, and it's so deep and intense and passionate, it feels like she's trying to tell me all the things she'd never say with words. The shocking intimacy of it is stunning, but it turns me on even more because I want it. I want her, and I want this, and I never want her to stop sucking on my tongue and nibbling on my lower lip and dragging her fingernails across my back and grinding down on me, and I never ever want to stop feeling her tits pressed against my chest, because *God,* this is heaven to me.

But this woman, she will never stop tantalizing me. She leans all the way back down to the mattress, letting her arms fall over her head and lifting her legs up to rest her ankles on my shoulders. I have no moral issues with this shift in positions, and I am plenty happy with the view, so I get on my knees, grab on to her thighs, and thrust harder and harder and deeper and deeper until she is crying out "Oh God, yes, Keaton, oh my God." This feels better than all the good things I've ever felt combined. Fucking hell, she's hot. I've never been so turned-on by a woman, and making her come for me is the only thing that matters now.

She's writhing and jerking around and gripping the sheets, and I keep going and going until I just can't anymore.

"Come inside me," she whispers. "It's okay."

Five words I did not expect to hear from her tonight,

and five seconds later, I do. I say her name just once and explode inside her, and the release is incredible.

Roxy fucking Carter.

I disappear into her and into myself and into the universe of me and her that I knew was out there, and if this is the only way in, well I can live with that.

I only get a glimpse of it, but it is glorious.

Before I fall asleep, I know without a doubt that I will do whatever it takes to get us back there, over and over.

CHAPTER 16
ROXY

"You look different. You look relaxed." My mother squints her eyes at her phone's camera.

"What? No. I just got some sun. Look at this view!" I turn my phone away from myself toward the view from the veranda. Keaton is inside, rolling calls with his assistant. It's early Monday morning, and I'm about to start dealing with some work stuff, but my parents just Skyped to check in with me.

"Why aren't you letting us see your face?" my mom asks. "What's going on? Is it the boy?"

"Shh!" I turn down the volume on my phone. "There's no 'the boy.'"

"Where is this boy?" My dad takes the phone from my mom. "What are we talking about?"

"Hey, Dad. Want to see the view?"

"Of what? The boy?"

"Of Antigua."

"Who?"

"Antigua. That's where I am now."

"Who are you there with?"

"Aimee and her husband. My friend Bernadette and her husband. And their...*our* friend Keaton."

"Keaton? You've never mentioned a Keaton," my mother says, swiping the phone from my dad.

"Keaton's a grown man, and that's his first name?" I hear my dad ask.

"Yes. He's a grown man. It's his first name."

"Sounds like a Mr. Hoity Toity Pretty Boy to me."

"He's Chase's best friend. I'm sure I've mentioned him."

"Is Keaton *the* boy?" my mom asks.

"Did someone say my name?" Keaton practically croons, stepping out onto the veranda.

I shake my head and try to wave him away.

"Put him on! Put him on the Skype! Where is he?" my mom yells.

Keaton strides over to stand right behind me, smiling into the camera over my shoulder. Half of each of my parents' faces are visible in the Skype window. "Good morning," he says, turning on the charm. "You must be Roxy's parents. I'm Keaton Bridges. Roxy's boyfriend. It's nice to Skype-meet you."

My mother squeals, "I knew it!" and covers her mouth, and my instinct is to throw my phone *and* Keaton over the railing.

"It's a couples-only resort," I explain, lowering my voice, "so Keaton and I have to pretend to be a couple and share a room. It's a whole thing, not a big deal."

"You're pretending to be Roxy's boyfriend *and* sharing a room with her?" my dad grunts. "Did you lose a bet?"

"I really feel like I've won the lottery," Keaton says, hand on heart.

Both of my parents guffaw at that.

"Please tell me there are two bathrooms!" my mom says.

"Actually, she's really started to pick up after herself." He pats me on the back. "She's a very considerate roommate."

"Really?" my mom asks. "Is she really? You're not just saying that? Because we couldn't wait to get her out of the house."

"So far I've found her to be very accommodating. And a great card player." He winks at them. Winks. At my parents.

"Oh, were you the one? Clever boy." My mom winks back at him.

Jesus.

"Who are you? The card game police? Thanks for blowing the lid off our parenting tricks," my dad mutters with a smirk. "You tell her about Santa Clause too?"

"I told her he won't be visiting this year if she doesn't tidy up her side of the bathroom counter."

"Hey, we should have tried that." My mom smacks my dad's arm, and the camera sways all over the place. I feel dizzy, but it might be because Keaton's hand has slid down to my ass, and I can't believe he's Skyping with my parents. This is so weird.

Keaton's phone vibrates, and he checks the Caller ID. "I am so sorry, but I have to take this call," he says to my parents. "I've really enjoyed talking to you, I hope to see you again soon." He sounds so earnest, I almost believe him.

"Nice to meet you, Keaton! Have fun with our girl!" My mother waves at him.

"It's impossible not to!" he calls out as he walks back inside and shuts the doors.

"He looks like the kinda guy who doesn't wear socks," my dad mutters.

Yeah. That's what I was expecting. My dad hates him. "How can you tell that just from seeing his face?"

"I know faces. I know feet."

"Well, he wears socks in the city. In public, anyway. I think."

"He looks like the kinda guy who could afford a lot of socks. Nice ones," my mother says. "You've never had a real boyfriend with a real job before."

"Yeah, well, I still haven't. He's not a real boyfriend."

"Well, anyway, you look well-rested. Are you actually sleeping in the same room with him? He sounds like a miracle worker."

"Mom! I gotta go! I have to make some work calls, and you guys have to leave for work soon, right?"

"Hey!" my dad says. "You be good to that guy, okay?"

"What?"

"You heard me. You think I don't know a guy who's crazy in love when I see one?"

"What are you talking about?"

"Oh, the way he was looking at you, Roxanne," my mother coos. "Didn't you see?"

"He's just pretending. We're pretending. Sometimes."

"I know faces. I know what the face of a man in love looks like," he says, and then he points to his own face. "It looks like this." He plants a quick kiss on my mother's cheek, making her squeal again and making the camera sway again, making me dizzy again, and then the Skype window closes.

As soon as I close that app, I see that I have a bunch of texts from Aimee, Bernadette, and Nina on our Girlfriends Group text, but I quickly realize that Aimee accidentally used the wrong group. She clearly meant to send Nina a message in their mommy group that I'm not a part of.

AIMEE: NINA! YOU. WILL. NOT. BELIEVE!!! K and R. It's a thing. It's happening.
NINA: STOP IT!!! Please tell me you're talking about Keaton and Roxy.
BERNADETTE: ROXTON is ON!!!
AIMEE: Do NOT let Roxy know that I told you because she's still being all weird about it— also don't let Chase know. Or Keaton. Better not tell Vince. Or Joni. In case our kids secretly text each other without our knowledge.
NINA: Got it. Dish!

AIMEE: They totally did it a couple of nights ago. Maybe last night too. Who knows probably. They're so cute, like seriously WTF, but I think it might actually work.
BERNADETTE: #ROXTON4EVA
NINA: Dying. So happy for them. Cannot believe I'm missing this, but I guess if we were there, then K and R wouldn't be, so yay for us!
ME: Hey guys. Wrong group text, but thanks for the support.
AIMEE: <wide-eyed blushing face emoji>
BERNADETTE: Busted!
NINA: Oh fudge me! Switching channels, sorry Rox. But you know...GET IT, GIRL! Xoxo

I put my phone to sleep and try to watch Keaton through the windows of the glass doors, but mostly I see my own reflection in them, and I'm shocked—shocked—to see the well-rested and relaxed face smiling back at me.

I open the doors and sit down in one of the Adirondack chairs, looking out at the view but listening to Keaton talk on the phone. It sounds like he's talking to one of his business partners about some investment opportunity. God, I love to hear him talk business. He's so confident and knowledgeable and authoritative. It's hot.

I close my eyes and let my head roll back as I

remember the way he let me touch him last night and the way he finally took control. The way he took control the night before. The way he keeps surprising me and challenging me and then giving me space when I need it. I've never been with a guy like that before. Oh God, the way he kissed me all over...

"Yeah. It was good, wasn't it?" he says, startling me.

I open my eyes and look up to find him grinning down at me.

"I was just listening to the waves."

"Were you? Because I was remembering what it felt like to have your hand on my—"

"Okay, okay. I need to start making some calls and dealing with things."

"Work stuff?"

"Work stuff." I look at my phone. "If you don't mind."

"Everything okay there?"

"Where?"

"Work. Is everything okay at work?" He takes a seat on the daybed, leaning forward and resting his elbows on his knees, and I can't stop staring at his forearms and hands and he knows it.

"Mostly."

"You sure?"

"I am a very competent and successful executive, you know."

"I do know that. You're the Senior Manager for Customer Relationship Management and Loyalty for the third largest online clothing store in America. So why are you putting up with shit from an employee?"

"You heard that?"

"Bits and pieces yesterday. Let me guess. You have a male employee who reports directly to you, but he went over your head for something and talked to your male boss about a matter that he should have come to you for."

"Yeah. He's done it twice now. I hired him four months ago."

"So what are you going to do about it?"

"I can handle it."

"Can you please tell me how you plan to handle it?"

"You don't think I can handle it?"

"I think you can handle anything. I would just like to offer my perspective on the situation if you'll let me. As a friend. Who happens to know and work with a lot of guys who have a problem with female superiors."

"Fine. This employee. We'll call him Bryce. Came highly recommended and he knows my superior—we'll call him Ansel—socially. He is perfectly good at his job, except for the part where he's supposed to respect my decisions. Twice now, he has disagreed with my strategy for a large-scale CRM program based on my data analysis of our performance metrics. When he brought it to my attention the first time, I thanked him for his opinion and told him I had made my decision and I had already presented it to the marketing department. He then went to Ansel privately to pitch him an alternative strategy. I only know this because Ansel mentioned in passing at lunch one day that Bryce had done this and that he didn't agree with him, but he did like the way he pitched it. On Friday, my assistant heard from Ansel's assistant that Bryce did it again, only he didn't bother to discuss it with me first because I was out of the office."

"And?"

"And I haven't heard from Ansel yet because of the weekend. Or possibly because he just doesn't plan on telling me."

"And what do you plan to do about Bryce?"

"I'm going to tell him I know what he did, that I appreciate feedback from my team, and I welcome anyone to challenge my tactics while we're at the development stage, but if he has a problem with my strategies, he needs to discuss it with me first."

"And?"

"And that's it. Believe it or not, I don't mouth off to people at work."

"Glad to hear it. Would you permit me to share my advice on another way to deal with it?"

"Yes. Fine. Tell me."

"You don't talk to Bryce first. You go to Ansel. You ask him to help you reinforce the chain of command. Use that phrase exactly. Maybe Ansel thought he was taking something off your plate by not bringing it up with you when it happened or by not telling Bryce it was inappropriate to go over your head. But you need Ansel to have your back and you want to make sure things work out with Bryce going forward. Say that."

"Uh-huh."

"Then you talk to Bryce. You tell him you know what he did and you ask him point blank why he didn't feel comfortable with your strategy or with coming to talk to you first. Just ask him why—don't put him on the defensive; don't be defensive. Thank him for his initiative and passion for the work and clarify your expectation for him to report to you directly about everything, regardless of his social relationship with Ansel. Ask him what you can do to make sure this doesn't happen again. Tell him what will happen if it happens again."

"I'll fire him."

"You fucking better. I'd fire him now, but I can be a dick like that."

"I'd like to think it's just a misunderstanding about protocol."

"I'd love to think that, but I'd put money on Bryce being a dick who wants your job."

"Yeah, well. That's some easy money right there." I shift around in my chair. I'd put money on me having Wet Panty Face right now, and that is very inconvenient because I really have to make some calls and I can't do that if Keaton's mouth is on my lady parts. Can I? "Okay. Thank you. For the advice."

"Any time. Literally." He looks at me, so seriously I can barely stand it. "I'm here for you, you know?"

"Okay."

"Okay." He stands up. "You gonna make your calls out here or in there or what? You want me around or no?"

"I mean..." I think about it for a second. "Yeah. You can be around. Sure. If you promise not to hop on the call and tell my boss you're my boyfriend."

"I'll try to refrain from interrupting your business calls, but I can't promise I won't shout it from the rooftops at some point."

I giggle.

Goddammit. He made me giggle again.

This guy.

I remember what my dad said and study his face and the way he's looking at me, and I guess it's so much easier to recognize a man who's crazy in love when he's looking at someone else, but whatever it is that Keaton is feeling, the way he's looking at me makes me feel better than I've felt in years. Or maybe ever.

CHAPTER 17
KEATON

W e're headed down the path for Game Night in the lobby, and I wait until Matt and Bernie and Chase and Aimee have entered the cottage before pulling Roxy back around a corner and surprising her with a kiss. She smells incredible and she looks so beautiful in a white dress with her golden skin, and I have earned this after helping her with her asshole employee situation. I have earned this after a day of not touching her while we lay out by the pool and on the beach, and also I just want to kiss her because I've been thinking about it all day.

Yeah, there's a word for what I was feeling, and it's German.

Vorfreude. The joyful anticipation of imagining something pleasurable or desired in the future.

I never would have anticipated feeling that way about this woman when I met her or for the many years since then. But goddammit, her response is even better than I imagined today. When I pull her toward me, one hand on her waist, one behind her neck, she reaches for my face and gives me one long kiss on the lips and then ten kisses all over my face like someone who's greeting a person she's been missing for a long time. Then she gives me one last quick kiss on the lips and walks away from me, going inside to join the others while I stand here wondering how it's possible that we haven't been in love with each other our whole lives.

I'm falling.

I'm falling hard and fast, and for now I don't even care if I'm heading down that path alone.

"Who is your man's favorite singer or band?" the resort manager asks.

Tonight, we're playing the Newlywed Game. When Roxy found out, she widened her eyes at me and whispered that maybe we should sit this one out. I assured her that it will be entertaining and she can just have fun with it if she doesn't know the answers. The six of us are all seated at the front of the room, guys on one side, ladies on the other, with half a dozen other couples and various resort employees sitting around watching us. We're all pretty much expecting Don and Debbie to win again, but you never know.

"We begin with an easy one," he says, winking at the ladies as he plays about ten seconds of some bouncy song from Herb Alpert and the Tijuana Brass on his phone.

I write down the name of my favorite musical artist on the little dry erase board and hold it so that no one can see it.

"Led Zeppelin!" Bernie yells out, barely even waiting for Matt to write the words down. He turns around his dry erase board, which says **Led**.

"One point for Matt and Bernadette!" the manager says and gives them a point on his scoreboard.

I thought Matt's favorite band was AC/DC, so I guess I'm a bad girlfriend.

Aimee smiles at her husband and says, "Chris Cornell."

Chase holds up his dry erase board, which has the words **Chris Cornell** scribbled on it, along with a vague doodle of a guy with long hair and a little facial scruff, and it basically looks like he did a self-portrait.

"One point for Chase and Aimee!"

That one I did know. I'm a good girlfriend to Chase.

I finally make eye contact with Roxy, who looks very unsure of herself, and I'm expecting her to say something like Shakira or Air Supply, but she kind of hums and then says, "Jay-Z?"

I smile and wink at her, flipping the board around.

She looks so happy that she got it right, it warms my heart.

"And one point for Keaton and Roxy! We are off to a good start tonight, ladies and gentlemen!" This manager guy really needs his own game show. "Second question, also easy. Ladies. What is your man's favorite alcoholic beverage?"

I write mine down and look up at Roxy, grinning. We haven't had many drinks *with* each other, but we've done a fair amount of drinking *around* each other over the years.

Bernie and Aimee easily score another point each with "gross expensive Scotch" and "Redbreast Irish whiskey."

Roxy declares confidently, "Gin and tonic."

"Close," I say as I turn my board around and reveal that an Old Fashioned is in fact my favorite.

"Really?" she says, disbelieving. Like I'd lie about that just to mess with her. She looks over at Aimee and mouths, *Did you know that?*

Aimee nods and whispers, "He drinks G&T when he needs to cheer up."

"Ahhh, new love," the manager says. "Still so much to learn about each other. An exciting time, not to worry. No point for you, though! Next question!"

Roxy blushes and exchanges a look with Aimee, not me. I catch Chase giving me the side-eye and give him an air kiss. My cock will not be blocked, and neither will my heart.

"This is a fun one, ladies! Which Disney princess is your man most attracted to?"

I don't have to think twice about that one, but Matt and Chase are making a big show of thinking it through.

"First to you, Lady Bernadette."

Bernie rolls her eyes. "He'll say it's Moana, but it's really Ariel."

Matt flips his board around to reveal that he did, in fact, write down ***Moana***. "It's Moana, and you can't prove otherwise."

"Oh yes, I can," she mutters. "But not here."

Aimee narrows her eyes at Chase. "He'll say Poca-hontas, but it's really Ariel."

Chase holds his answer up—**Pocahontas, but she thinks it's the Little Mermaid**. "Innocent until proven guilty, babe."

"I know what I know, babe."

"Points for Bernadette's and Aimee's teams! What does Roxy say?"

"Roxy says it's the Little Mermaid and he has no reason to lie about it." She shrugs. "I'd do her."

I do not need the image of Roxy doin' the Little Mermaid in my head right now, but I fully expect to get a slap-down as soon as she sees my answer.

"*Princess Leia?*" she snaps. "She's not a Disney princess!"

"Disney now owns the franchise. And she is a princess."

"No point for Roxy's team!"

"Am I allowed to change my answer?" Matt asks.

"Me too," Chase says.

Roxy's eyes are ablaze, but not with anger. She likes my answer. I bet she'd do Princess Leia too.

"Next question!" The manager turns on the Herb Alpert song again. "What movie is guaranteed to make your man cry?"

I swear, all three of us are tearing up just thinking about our answers.

"*Marley and Me*," Bernie says, pouting, and she's right.

Aimee correctly guesses "*E.T.*"

Roxy says, "*Pretty Woman*" with a definitive nod, because she would have no idea and she expects to guess wrong anyway at this point.

Toy Story 3 is what I wrote down, ***but Roxy will probably say Pretty Woman***.

It gets a laugh from everyone, including Roxy, whose expression also conveys disbelief and fondness and just the right amount of lust for the occasion.

"Do we get anything for that?" she asks the manager.

"Half a point for Roxy's team!"

She comes over to high-five me. "We're half right!"

"We're all right," I say under my breath. "You just don't know it yet."

That gets me a confused look when she sits back down.

"Final question for the ladies, and then we switch over! This one is multiple choice. What does your man irrationally fear the most? One, sharks. Two, ghosts. Three, intimacy. Four, fill in the blank."

Everyone knows that Matt has a fear of sharks because he grew up surfing, although I'm pretty sure he's more afraid of belly fat.

Aimee reveals that Chase is irrationally afraid someone will shave off his beautiful wavy hair while he's sleeping. At a certain time in our lives, I'm pretty sure that someone was me, and I'll be honest, I did consider it when we were in college. But look how far we've come.

"And back to you, Miss Roxy," the manager says with a wink. I'm starting to think he has a thing for her. "What is Mr. Keaton irrationally afraid of?"

"Socks," she says.

I have to laugh at that as I flip my board around.

"Really?" Roxy is skeptical. "Really? *You* are afraid of ghosts?"

"Well, technically I've been afraid of being haunted by a demon ever since I saw *Paranormal Activity*."

"No point for Roxy and Keaton! Gentlemen! Give your dry erase boards to your ladies, please!"

I get up to hand the dry erase board, eraser, and pen to Roxy. As she takes them in her hands, she slowly leans in, and I wait for her to kiss my cheek, but she says, "Boo!" and then sits back in her chair, grinning.

You don't scare me, Roxy Carter.

"Gentlemen!" the manager says. "Let's see how well you know your women! Easy questions first again. Tell us her favorite singer or band!" He plays that ridiculous Herb Alpert song again, but it doesn't bother me.

I don't need another second to come up with the answer.

Roxy finishes writing, pops the cap back on the pen, and arches an eyebrow at me, grinning.

I am surprised to learn that Bernie's favorite singer is Patti Smith, but Matt knew.

Chase reluctantly admits that his wife's favorite band is The Chainsmokers, and this is basically the biggest conflict in their relationship.

Roxy turns her attention to me. She's clutching the sides of the dry erase board, and I can tell she's just waiting to say, "*Hah*! Wrong!"

Sorry, baby.

"Roxy's favorite singer is Bruce Springsteen."

Roxy's face falls, and she looks down to check to make sure I couldn't see what she had written. I couldn't. I know she loves the Boss. I know she loves him because her dad loves him. It's unexpected and it used to be one of my favorite things about her, until I suddenly developed about twenty favorite things. The thing about people who love Bruce Springsteen is they never shut up about it once someone gets them talking about him. She just never realized I was listening.

She flips the dry erase board around, and the resort manager also appears shocked that I got it right.

"One point for Keaton and Roxy!"

Roxy keeps her eyes on me while she erases the words ***Bruce freakin' Springsteen!*** from the board. I hold her gaze for as long as she can handle it.

"Now. Gentlemen. For another easy point. Tell us her favorite alcoholic drink!"

Literally everyone in the room knows that Bernie's favorite beverage is red wine because she's had a glass of it in her hand every night we've been here and she's sipping from one right now.

Chase is proud to declare that his wife now has the same favorite drink as him.

I rub my chin with my fingers and pause to add a little dramatic flair, and then I say, "She probably wrote Blue Moon beer because that's her favorite to drink when she's just hanging out. But when she really wants to have fun, she needs something with tequila in it. Around the holidays she's up for hot chocolate with literally any kind of alcohol in it, any time of day. The only red wine she'll drink is Malbec. Champagne goes straight to her head and her heart, so she'll only drink it at weddings. But she drinks a lot of it. Did I leave anything out, babe?"

She shakes her head as she turns the board around. It

says ***Blue Moon.*** Hesitantly apologetic ice blue eyes meet mine, but her little smile is giving me life.

"Another point for Mr. Keaton and Ms. Roxy! And now...men...A hypothetical question... If your woman can marry a superhero, which one would she choose?"

Matt predicts his wife would answer Harry Potter, even though he isn't technically a superhero—but he is wrong. Bernie wants to marry Loki. "Loki's not a super-hero either," he says, rolling his eyes.

"Well, I'm going to marry him anyway." She shrugs.

"No point for Mr. Matt and Mrs. Bernadette. Oh, too bad! To you, Mr. McKay!"

Chase narrows his eyes at his wife and says, "She wants to marry Loki too, even though he is not a superhero."

Aimee holds her board up in front of her face and says, "But I love him almost as much as I love you!"

"A point for Mr. and Mrs. McKay, and two points for Mr. Loki! Mr. Keaton, what say you?"

I shrug. "I'm going with Loki, even though he is defi-nitely not a superhero."

Roxy holds her board up and says to Aimee and Bernie, "He's mine. Loki is mine."

"Three points for Loki, and one more point for Keaton and Roxy. My goodness," the manager says.

Roxy gives me a little smirk as she erases ***Loki + Roxy = TLF*** from the board.

Fuck you, Loki. Roxy is mine.

"Next question! To the men... Which actress would

your lady cast as herself in the romantic comedy movie of your relationship?"

We all laugh because that is a stellar question, but Roxy doesn't break eye contact with me while she writes down her answer. It's almost as if she's hoping I'll get this one right.

Matt stares at his wife while he slowly answers, "I would cast Zooey Deschanel or Emma Stone, but I think Bernie would cast...Lucille Ball."

Bernie's face erupts in a smile as she flips her board around to reveal that she wrote *Lucy!!!*

Chase correctly answers that Aimee would want Jennifer Garner to play herself, and I would definitely watch that movie.

I'm not a mind reader, but I am an excellent poker player and a good dealmaker, so I can figure out how people's minds work in certain situations. In this one, Roxy wants me to keep this winning streak going, so it's not about who she'd really cast as herself—she's trying to make this easy for me. And she likes to think we're so different from each other. And that she's a wise-cracking hooker with a heart of gold.

"Julia Roberts," I say.

She looks relieved as she confirms that I am indeed a genius who understands her.

"What do you know, folks! Another point for Keaton and Roxy's team. Moving on! Final question for this group... What does your woman have an irrational fear of? A, spiders? B, being stuck in an elevator with your mother? C, intimacy? D, fill in the blank."

The music plays, and I watch Roxy put some thought into this one.

"Mr. Matt McGovern! What does your lovely wife have an irrational fear of?"

Matt scratches his chin while staring at his lovely wife. "Well, she used to have a fear of intimacy *and* a fear of flu shots, but now I think it's safe to say she only has an irrational fear of flu shots."

Bernie flips her board around, and they get another point. "It's only irrational until somebody dies," she says, frowning and polishing off her glass of wine.

Chase and Aimee have been laughing ever since the guy asked the question, because everyone who knows Aimee knows that she has an irrational fear of a zombie apocalypse.

"It's only irrational until somebody dies and then comes back to life and wants to eat your brain," Aimee says.

"It's irrational because I would never let that happen," Chase assures everyone.

"Mr. Keaton. Share with us your guess for Roxy's irrational fear."

Roxy tries to keep her expression as neutral as possible while I study her. Up until yesterday, I would not have hesitated to say she fears intimacy, and neither would she. But right now... "I think she has an irrational fear of subway grates."

Roxy's jaw drops, and then her eyes well up with tears. "How did you know that?" she says, barely loud enough for me to hear.

"I've noticed you always walk around them," I tell

her, like it's no big deal. But it obviously is a big deal to her. And to Aimee and Bernie, who are both looking at me with wet eyes and pouty lips.

I am seriously considering going back to acting like a self-centered asshole, because this is not the kind of female attention that I'm comfortable with.

"One big *how did he know that* point for Team Keaton and Roxy! Now if the next group would come up please, and let's have a round of applause for this one!" He plays an applause sound effect on his phone. This guy.

When we walk over to take a seat on a sofa, Roxy says quietly, shaking her head. "I am so confused right now."

"About?"

She turns to face me. "I can't tell if you're trying to fuck with me or if you..."

"If I what?"

"If you just *know* me."

"I am definitely not trying to fuck with you, Roxanne." My hand reaches for her face, just as I feel Chase's hand slap my back.

"Well-played, guys. Good game."

Roxy and I laugh and take a step away from each other, and Chase's hand slides up to the back of my neck, half strangling it.

"We can't all be a perfect couple," I say.

"I'm getting Aimee a drink—Rox, you want anything?"

"I'm good. Thanks, Dad."

Chase pulls me aside, to the table with the refreshments and snacks. "You slept with her, didn't you?"

"You must have me confused with someone who is not a gentleman."

"Not cool, dude."

"Ever occur to you that I might be the one who's in trouble here?"

Chase smiles as he pops a banana chip into his mouth and pats me on the back, reassuringly this time. "Ever occur to you that that's what I was worried about all along?"

"Should we grab a drink at the bar?" Roxy nudges my shoulder as we reach the conjunction of paths to the cottages and the bar.

I nod toward our friends. "I think they're all going back to their cottages."

"That's okay. I meant just us."

Just us.

Those two little words are as delicate and meaningful as a soft kiss on the cheek from this woman.

"Yeah. Let's grab a drink."

"First Old Fashioned is on me." She takes my hand, and out of the corner of my eye, I can see her examining the profile of my face as we veer off the path toward the bar. "Tell me about yourself, Keaton Bridges," she says.

Chase and Aimee may have won Game Night, but I am winning Roxy Carter's heart.

CHAPTER 18
ROXY

Have you always been this handsome? I am thinking as I suck more of this inspired rum cocktail into my mouth through two little green straws while leaning across the little table toward him.

"What's your favorite color?" is what I ask him.

"Ice blue," he says, staring into my eyes.

"Uh-huh. And is it brown when you're staring into the eyes of a brown-eyed girl?"

"My favorite color is now ice blue," he states, very convincingly, as he takes a sip of his Old Fashioned.

Apparently every other couple at this resort has already retired to their cottage, because Keaton and I are the only ones at the bar, so we have the deck to ourselves, we have the friendly bartender to ourselves, we have the twinkling hurricane candleholders to ourselves, we have the sound of the waves below and the dreamy steel drum music from the hidden speakers to ourselves, and we have this *samar* all to ourselves.

I may not have been able to answer every question about Keaton Bridges in a room full of people, but I can ask him every question and I can give him this. This night. My time. My full attention. And my sudden inability to let go of his big, beautiful hand. God, it's so dumb. A warm breeze carries his clean, masculine scent in my direction, and I inhale shamelessly.

Why do I feel the urge to slather myself in cocoa butter and walk around naked in front of you until you drop to your knees?

"What's your favorite kung fu movie?"

He lowers the tumbler and twirls it so the ice cubes clink against the glass. "It's a three-way tie. I love *Crouching Tiger* for a lot of reasons, but there's this little movie from Hong Kong called *Ip Man* that's a biopic about the master who taught Bruce Lee, and also..." He grins. "I really fucking love *The Karate Kid*. It's not exactly a kung fu movie, but it's the first movie I saw with martial arts in it, and it's what made me want to watch more."

"I love *The Karate Kid* too. I mean, not the sequel to *The Karate Kid*, but I also love that movie."

"I'm gonna make you watch all of my favorites with Finn and me."

I take another big sip of this delicious fruity island love potion before saying, "I think I would actually enjoy that."

"I am completely certain that you will."

"How do you know so much about me?" I marvel.

"I told you," he says, two lines appearing between his perfectly groomed eyebrows. "I've always thought of you as a friend. You've been a part of my inner circle for a long time. Whether you realized it or not."

My stupid nose is tingling again, for like the fifth time tonight.

When did you become this person that I could actually love?

"What were you like when you were a kid?"

He looks down and laughs, kind of a sad little laugh.

Why have I never noticed how long your eyelashes are?

"I just remember being needy and lonely most of the time, until I was about eight. My dad was always working and traveling, and my mom—she's a nice person, but she's always been involved in fundraising for charities and museums, so she was busy. I mean, I had friends once I was in preschool, but before then I had Nanny Rey."

"Right." I nod. Of course he had a nanny.

"Her name was Reyna, but I guess I had trouble pronouncing it at first, or maybe I just didn't want to. She was this beautiful Filipino woman. Probably in her thirties. So kind and sweet but tough with me when I was being a little shit. She was the one who took me to school and everywhere, and I worshipped her. When I was old enough, she told me she had a son who was older than me, back in the Philippines, who she had to give up for adoption when she was a teenager. I was so jealous of him because I knew she'd rather be with him than me. One day my mom told me that the adoption agency had contacted Reyna and put her son in touch with her and that she'd be moving back to the Philippines. I was nine and I didn't really need a nanny at that point, but I thought my life was over."

Why do I feel the sudden urge to take you home and make you dinner? "She went back to her son?"

"She left me. No wait—you're right. She went back to her son. That's what I learned in the five therapy sessions my mom made me go to after Reyna left. After that I had to learn to get better at making friends, so I did. I got awesome."

"You learned how to be charming."

"Oh, you noticed."

"Sometimes. Did she stay in touch with you? Reyna?"

"She sent me letters at first, yeah. I sent her cards and a lot of pictures of myself. But you know, eventually the letters stopped coming. It's fine. She was happy. I was happy for her. Eventually."

"What's that Russian word? *Uzbliuto*?"

"*Razbliuto*. I wouldn't call it that, though. I still love her. I'm sure I'll never see her again, but it wasn't the kind of love you fall out of. It's more of a *saudade* situation."

"*Saudade*," I repeat.

"Yeah. It's one of those. A love that remains. A longing." He leans forward to brush away the hair that's blown across my face, and I lean my cheek against his hand.

"Tell me about your parents," I say. "You're not allowed to say you don't want to talk about them this time."

He drains his glass and signals to the waiter that we

need another round. "Okay, but I need another drink. That all right?"

"We can close the place down if you want to."

"I want to do a lot of things right now, Rox. But all of them involve you."

I polish off the last of my rum happy juice before I'm capable of saying, "I want to do a lot of things with you too. But I want to know more about you first."

He smiles and squeezes my hand. "Thank you."

"Oh God, don't thank me."

"It means a lot to me. More than you know."

The bartender brings our drinks over himself. "Anything else for the lovers? They will be closing down the kitchen very soon."

"What do you want, lover?" Keaton asks me with a smile and a wink.

Oh God, I want to sit on your lap and kiss you and never stop.

I want to make up for so much lost time with you.

I want you to know that I'm not really a dick, because now I know for a fact that you are not one.

"I'm good" is all I say to him. "Thank you," I say to the bartender.

After he's had a few sips of his second Old Fashioned, while still holding my hand across the table, Keaton exhales loudly and says, "My mom—Cynthia Harrington Bridges—as I mentioned, is a nice lady. She's not exactly maternal, but she always means well, and she was just raised to be a good wife and daughter more than anything, I think. She likes to give me things. Gifts. That's her way of showing me she cares. Always has been. My dad—William Bridges—is a self-made man. My mom comes from money, and my dad made his first million by the time he was twenty-two. He's an investor. He really is like Richard Gere in *Pretty Woman*. He buys companies in hostile takeovers and then breaks them down to sell for a profit. He's not a bad guy. He's even a pretty good person, I'd say. He's just not a great father. I never resented him for it, I just used to want his approval so much, it was...exhausting."

"And you don't anymore?"

He shakes his head thoughtfully while twirling his glass again. "I'm not as rich as he is, but he would always tell me how much money he had made by the time he was thirty, like it was the measure by which he judged all men. So by the time I turned thirty and I realized that I had made as much money as he had by the time he was thirty, I realized it wasn't that big of a deal. And I kinda felt bad for him. Because I have what he doesn't have and probably never will. I have good friends. Great ones."

That's when I finally lift my ass up from my chair and lean over the table to kiss him on the mouth.

Not kissing this man is no longer an option.

I kiss him until I've taken his breath away and then given it back to him.

I sit back down and watch him rub his lips together, savoring the taste of me and my rum and pineapple-laced lip gloss.

"Go on," I say.

His dimple makes a welcome appearance as he tries to speak again. "Umm... What was I saying?"

"You have good friends. Great ones."

"I do. And I'd say that I'm a lot closer to Chase's parents now. Have been for years, really."

"Graziella and Sean?" I say, smiling. Because no one can think about those two wonderful people without smiling. "I love them. I love their restaurant. I haven't seen them since New Year's Eve." I'm hit with a pang of regret when I think about how hard I was trying to avoid him that night. I left before he showed up. What if I'd stayed? Would we have had a midnight kiss? Would we be a real couple by now?

"We should have dinner at their restaurant together sometime," he says. "It would blow their minds."

It would blow my mind too. I can't quite picture being with Keaton in Brooklyn yet. But I'm willing to.

The next question rushes out to greet him before I can stop it. "Do you want kids?"

"Hell yeah," he says without hesitating. "A brood. Or half a brood, I don't know. How big is a brood? I want at least three."

That revelation punches me right in the ovaries. "Three, huh?"

"I just want to be a better dad than mine was, and I'm afraid I'll screw things up with the first one."

I can't help but laugh at that. "So—what? The first-born is just a screwed-up guinea pig? That's not fair. Although I am slightly more awesome than my brother is, so you have a point."

"Are you saying you think three is too many?"

I find myself swallowing hard and shifting around in my chair and doing some sort of gynecological math in my head... Nope. Numbers and years aren't making sense to me right now. "I mean. I'd be happy with one. I'd be fine with screwing things up with one kid."

He nods once. "Yeah. You'll be good at that."

"Screwing up a kid?"

"Yeah."

"Thanks."

"We will, I mean." He twists his lips to the side. "Too much? Too soon?"

He leans across the table and kisses me until I've forgotten what the hell he just said.

What did anyone just say?

What are words again?

This man has snuck up on me faster than a coconut full of Caribbean rum cocktail. I am giddy and holding on to this wonderful feeling before the vomit and regret kicks in. Shit, I'm probably going to snore again tonight.

My next question stumbles out of my mouth like a drunk girl from an Uber: "Why did you and Tamara break up?"

He blinks, surprised, and it takes him a second to respond to that one. "She moved to LA, and she didn't want me to go with her."

"Yeah, but...I mean, you don't have to tell me if you don't want to...but why didn't she want you to go with her? You're great."

"I don't know why exactly. She said she wanted to start a new chapter in her life, and she didn't think she could do it with me."

"You really loved her."

"I don't really want to talk about her with you. Not

now, anyway. This is the good part. I don't want to think about the bad stuff when I'm with you."

He lifts my hand and presses it to his lips. Of all his kisses, this might be the one that does me in because I can actually see his face while he's kissing me and he really means it. He means this kiss. I mean something to him, and he means something to me, and the only thing I want to dropkick is my brain because it can barely stay awake and I'm not ready to sleep. I'm not ready for this feeling or this night or this vacation to be over.

I'm not sure if I'm really ready for Keaton yet, but I am definitely here for the good part.

CHAPTER 19
KEATON

We didn't exactly close the bar down last night, but we did return to the cottage to talk on the veranda until after midnight and then fall asleep in each other's arms on top of the covers, fully clothed. One of us snored and one of us was so tired and happy it didn't even keep him awake. One of us woke up in the middle of the night and shook the bed, pretending to be terrified of something she said she heard in the bathroom, made the other get up to check, and when he did—because he's a brave-as-balls stud who would do anything to protect a woman he cares about— she ran outside to the doors between the shower and the veranda and started rattling them. The way a ghost demon would rattle doors.

One of us nearly lost his shit in a badass sexy masculine way, and if the other one ever tells anyone about it, it will be the last obnoxious thing she ever says.

But I think she scared the irrational fear right out of me.

And I had to admit it was really fucking funny once I'd calmed down.

We got back in bed and laughed until we fell asleep again. It was a no-sex night, but I feel closer to her than ever. And now I get to see if she goes one step forward, two steps back. The bathroom door is closed, and I can hear Roxy moving around in there. I reach for my phone on the bedside table, and I'm reminded that it's February fourteenth. It's after nine, so when I hear the polite knock at the front door, I get up quickly, knowing it's probably the flowers I ordered from the concierge right after we got here—and not a ghost demon.

Sure enough, I'm faced with a massive arrangement of exotic local blooms, so big I can barely see the top of the head of the young man who's holding it. I take the giant vase from him and tell him to wait so I can put it on the bench inside and grab a tip from my wallet. Then he holds out the other thing that I ordered from the concierge after our first night here—a little gift bag filled with nasal strips and ear plugs. Just a little something for my bedmate so she knows I'm not just giving her a generic awesome flower gift for Valentine's Day.

I go out to the veranda to stretch and breathe in the fresh air and then take a seat on the daybed to look at the pictures the dog hotel sent me last night and respond to a few emails. After a couple of minutes, I realize the veranda doors to the shower are slowly swinging open. My first thought is that Roxy is trying to scare the shit out of me again, and my next thought is—nothing. My mind goes blank, because twenty feet away from me, Roxy is standing in the shower completely naked. She is standing with her back to me, running her hands over herself as water streams down her body, and it is the sexiest damn thing I have ever seen. Until she turns to face me.

She isn't oiled-up, but she is wet and glistening and stunning, and there aren't enough flowers in the world to equal this Valentine's Day gift. Her eyes beckon me to join her, and I somehow manage to stand and walk over to her. I'd call this three steps forward, no steps back. I don't know how I'm managing to casually stroll toward her as if this isn't the best thing that's ever happened to me, I just hope I don't collapse to the ground before I get to touch her, but I'd die a happy man, nonetheless.

I stop to remove my clothing and shut the doors behind me, because one of us will be screaming out the other's name very soon, and I want it to be her. I want her. Jesus, I want to do all the things, for and with and to her.

"That's one helluva body you've got there, Carter." I stare down at her neck and her collarbone and her full breasts and pink nipples.

"I'm growing rather fond of yours too," she says as her hands reach for my chest.

"I always knew you would."

"I will do whatever you want me to do to it in this shower for the next ten minutes, but then we have to turn off the water because it's a limited resource, even on an island."

Fucking hell, Shower Roxy is just as hot and wonderful as I'd imagined she would be and twice as eco-friendly.

I grit my teeth as those very confident hands slowly

slide down the front of me. "That is a very generous offer." I grab on to her wrists. "But you can do whatever you want to my body for the rest of my life, as far as I'm concerned." I place her hands, crossed, behind the small of her back so I can see the gentle slope of her waist to her hips and the way her belly is somehow flat but soft and so inviting. "And for the next ten minutes, I'm going to do what *your* body wants me to do to it."

Her response is something between a sigh and a moan and a grunt, and it's better and more meaningful than any word in any language.

I do what any man would do for this woman: I kneel before her, and I will be the only man who does this for the rest of her life.

I grip her hips and turn her to face the tiled wall so she can hold on to it for support, because she'll need it. But she does what no woman has ever done for me before —she slowly bends forward at the waist, to hold on to her ankles...and fuuuuuck me, *this* is the best thing that has ever happened to me or possibly to anyone ever.

I am the luckiest man alive, but the planet just got lucky too because this shower sex is going to be dirtier and over a lot quicker than I had anticipated. I groan and squeeze her ass and drive my tongue into her, and I fuck her with my tongue, relentlessly, and I don't let up until after she's done screaming, "Keaton! Oh God, Keaton!" and crying out like she's in pain, but she's not in pain. I am. When she's gone silent and limp, I slowly stand and help her up, turning her to face me again and kissing her until she's got the fire back in her.

I press her up against the wall and press myself up

against her, and I am the king of the world when she lifts one leg and wraps it around me, and I press my impatient cock up inside her, and my name on her lips becomes a gasp and then exuberant panting with my vigorous thrusts and then back to some breathless hint of my name over and over again.

Everything is wet and warm and hard and soft and delirious but also completely in focus.

I keep going for as long as I can, but when I come, it's intense and blinding.

When we've both caught our breath, she kisses me on the mouth and reaches out to pump shower gel into her hand and she washes me clean. It's beautiful and humbling and empowering, and it's all over so quickly, but we're both so eager to collapse back onto the bed and lie there in each other's arms.

We drift in and out of consciousness for hours, exhausted in the way that you are when you're becoming something new. I am fully aware of how confused and hesitant she is sometimes when we wake up to move our arms and legs around and she looks at me, all heavy-lidded and bleary-eyed. But I can also see her trying to push through whatever fear is left.

It's almost noon when we finally get up and decide to head down to the restaurant, and I'm ready to give her the other Valentine's Day gift I've been dying to give her.

Roxy is alternately shy and her usual sasshole self over lunch. We both comment how we feel like everyone is eyeing us like they heard us sex-screaming earlier. Even if they had, it can't be anything they haven't heard before around here, and surely we would have gotten texts from our friends—who have been notably quiet text-wise so far today and are definitely absent from the common areas of the resort.

"Why do you keep grinning at me?"

"I have something for you."

"Again? That's not fair. I didn't get you anything."

"Oh, but you gave me something that I will treasure forever."

She blushes and covers her face. "All right, all right. What is it?"

"A nickname."

She peeks through her fingers. "It better not have anything to do with what we did this morning."

"Everything has something to do with what we did this morning."

She tosses half a dinner roll at me. I catch it and return it to the basket.

"This is just my personal nickname for you—it's not going to catch on like Franzia or Foxy Roxy. It's kind of a thinker."

"Oh my God, just tell me already."

"It's Ute. It's short for the Norwegian word *Utepils*. It means sitting outside on a sunny day, enjoying a beer, but more specifically it's the first beer you drink outside on a sunny day after a long harsh winter. That's how I feel about you. How I've been feeling about you. Or more like, I'll always look forward to having that feeling with you. There are these moments, when it's like once the snow finally melts and there's just nothing more satisfying than having a nice cold beer outside in the sun. I've never felt that with anyone else. I like it."

In the long silence that follows, a less confident man would probably expect her to roll her eyes and walk away. But I know better. I know I'm waiting for that ray of sunshine.

She finally blinks, takes a sip of water, slams the glass back down, and says, "I like it. The nickname. Ute. And I like you."

"Good. I like you too."

"Fuckin' A."

She takes a big bite of her sandwich, shoves a few fries into her mouth, and then says, "This is hopelessly crazy, you know? Me and you?"

"I respectfully disagree. I think it was always only a matter of time."

"What if it's just a vacation thing?"

"What if it isn't?"

"What if it doesn't work out? What if we go back to hating each other when we get back to Brooklyn?"

"I never really hated you, and that's kind of the point of dating. To see if it works out."

"You hated me."

"I had complicated feelings regarding your manner of behavior toward me at first, sure."

She gasps dramatically and then leans forward, lowering her voice. "Did you want to hate-fuck me?"

"*Did* I? I want to hate-fuck you right now."

Our waitress comes by, all smiles. "How is everything? Can I get you anything else?"

"We're good, thank you. It's delicious," Roxy says.

"We definitely have everything we need here, thank you."

Roxy waits for the waitress to walk away and then lowers her voice again. "Speak for yourself."

"You really can't admit that I'm enough for you? Have you not had your fill of Tads and musicians? Oh by the way, I asked Aimee about your boyfriends."

"I know."

"Interesting."

She wipes her mouth with her napkin, grips the edge of her chair, and narrows her eyes at me. "Are you saying you can't play an instrument?"

"Baby, I will become the next drummer for the E Street Band if that's what it takes to get you to take me seriously, but I don't believe that's what you want at this point in your life."

She rubs her lips together, and I can tell, even though I can't see through the table, that she is rubbing her thighs together too. "You done eating?"

"You want me to take you back to bed?" I take my napkin from my lap and place it on the table. "I'm done."

"Good. Let's go."

I leave a tip for the waitress, signal to her to charge everything to the room, and we're heading out of the restaurant in three seconds.

"Would you really learn to play the drums for me?" she asks as she takes my hand.

"I mean. If I learn to play the drums, it would have to be for the benefit of all the ladies. If it makes you dig me more, that's a bonus."

"Would you dig me more if I wear a pearl necklace and a headband?"

"I don't think I could possibly dig you any more, but if that's all you're wearing, then it wouldn't hurt."

"I think it's safe to say I'm falling in love with her," I say to Chase and Matt as we're walking down to the resort's nightclub. "Hard."

Chase pats me on the back. "How's she treating you?"

I exhale slowly as I stare at the ground and shove my hands into my pockets. "Pretty much how you'd expect. And also in the most surprising ways imaginable."

"You should try *converge-sating* with her," Matt offers.

"What?"

"It's this thing that Bernie's parents do, and we've done it a few times. It's where you both talk about your shit until you sort of merge with the other person. It's not as bad as it sounds."

"I'm not doing that."

"Fair enough."

CHAPTER 20
ROXY

"'m falling for him. Hard," I mutter to Aimee and Bernadette. We're walking twenty paces behind the guys as we make our way down to the nightclub. "It's insane. It's so hopelessly crazy." And I can't believe I'm having this conversation on Valentine's Day—the dumbest day of the year.

Aimee squeezes my arm. "Dude. If there's a zombie apocalypse, Keaton would totally pay someone to protect you."

"He's such a good guy now. What are you afraid of?" Bernadette asks.

"It's not Keaton I'm afraid of, so much as who I'll be if I'm with him."

Bernadette screws up her face. "Mrs. Bridges?"

"A mess."

"Being vulnerable is not the same as being a mess," Aimee insists.

"It is the way I do it. Don't you remember?"

She shakes her head slowly. Of course she doesn't

remember. Why would she? She's had a career and a husband and a kid since then.

"It's not that I don't remember the way you were, Rox, it's that I see who you are now. And I see who Keaton is now. And I can't even stand the thought of the two of you not really being together anymore."

I place my hands on my butterfly-filled belly. "Me neither. It's all happening so fast."

"Is it? Or has it been happening incredibly slowly for years and years?" Bernadette says.

"That's kind of what he said."

"I wonder if we should tell Chase now," Aimee whispers.

As soon as she says it, Chase pats Keaton on the back and turns to walk toward us, looking at me. I stop in my tracks, like *oh shit, Dad found out I had sex —hide me!*

"Can I talk to you for a second, Rox?" he asks while pulling his wallet out from his back pocket.

"I would like to request your wife's presence."

He rolls his eyes. "I'm not mad or anything. I know about you and Keaton—I'm happy for you."

"Aww." Aimee rubs her husband's shoulder. "See you guys inside."

Chase pulls a small faded-yellow card out of his wallet and stares down at it while sliding the wallet back into his pocket. "This is from the Zoltar Speaks machine in Coney Island." He holds it up and then hands it over to me.

It says: ***You may be riding the winds of change. Things may at times seem to be out of***

touch. Soon they will come down to a better order.

"Aimee got it that first night we spent together, and she gave it to me when I had fallen for her but I was thinking that we had to pump the brakes while she was working in our offices. And Keaton was...you know the story."

"Yes, I do."

"I've kept it in my wallet ever since then, to remind myself not to get too caught up in whatever my brain is telling me when it comes to matters of the heart. You're the last person I ever thought would need this more than I do. And I guess Keaton was the last person I ever thought you'd be riding the winds of change with...but I don't know anyone who's changed as much as he has over the years. For the better. There is nothing that guy wouldn't do for the people he loves, and I'd tell anyone the same about you. So whatever little love-hate, push-pull song and dance you've got going on in that head of yours...it's time to find another rhythm. Know what I mean?"

I slip the card inside my bra, wipe the stupid solitary tear that's formed in the corner of my eye, and nod.

He gives my arm a little punch as he holds the door to the nightclub open for me. "You got this."

I walk through that door and straight over to Keaton, who's standing at the bar, surrounded by our best friends, and I take his face in my hands and kiss him on the mouth. I kiss him in front of our friends and the bartender and the band and the good people of The Coco

Beach Resort. I'm done pretending that he's not really my boyfriend.

By the time I've finally detached my lips from his, Keaton is the one who's a little wobbly for a change, and our friends are all out on the dance floor. I take his hand and lead him out there to join them. The house band is some kind of fusion of Calypso, rock, and island beats. I don't know what to call it, but it's happy and it's impossible not to move your body to it.

Unless you're Matt McGovern. I have never seen Matt McGovern dance before—and I still haven't. He's basically just standing there looking hot and laughing while Bernie holds his hand and does some kind of salsa step around him. Chase and Aimee are their usual sexy cool selves—although they really can't compete with Don and Debbie, who are practically doing the horizontal mambo and putting us all to shame.

When I'm still facing away from Keaton, I close my eyes, say a silent prayer to the gods of dance and new love, and hope that this man's dick doesn't shrivel up and crawl back up inside him when he sees me dance in the only way I've ever known how. But before I can let go of his hand and start swinging my arms vehemently, twisting and jumping while kicking the air, he spins me around and takes both of my hands, holding them up about chest height. He sways his hips a little and steps back and forth, and I just follow. I don't know if this is salsa, mambo, samba, or some new thing that he's making up just for me, but it feels right and I can do this. I can't even tell if he's leading or not. I just know that I'm willing to follow him and see where this goes.

CHAPTER 21
KEATON

We had one perfect day together yesterday in Antigua.

A day of lying out on the veranda naked. A day of lounging in our private plunge pool naked. A day of bathing in our outdoor bathtub together naked.

We napped in each other's arms on a hammock with a view of the beach—fully clothed.

We had one epic dinner in town with our friends—three real couples with amazing tans who were enjoying each other's company and the final hours of warm salty air and a slow pace before returning to an icy, slushy hellscape where everyone is battered by relentless noise, rushing to get everywhere, and constantly aware of never having enough of anything when you get there.

Except us.

Roxy and I are in the bubble.

There's a Norwegian word for this phase that we're

in: *forelsket*. That feeling of euphoria when you're falling in love.

I went to a cocktail party once where they served chocolate-covered candied ginger as a snack. That's what Roxy reminds me of now. Sweet and zingy with a hint of spice and fire. Satisfying and mouthwatering and absolutely fucking perfect.

We held hands the entire plane ride back. Her fingers spoke of love while her big sexy mouth expelled mostly sarcasm and sass. But with every snarky comment, there's a twinkle in her ice blue eyes, like some fairy that got stuck beneath a frozen Siberian lake.

I'd love to say that we're too happy to notice how fucking cold it is when we land in Newark, but it is really fucking cold.

Manny carries our luggage to the car, and I pick up Roxy. She doesn't have her winter boots with her, and I think she's much lighter now that she isn't holding all that sexual tension and resistance to my awesomeness in her muscles.

"What are you doing?"

"Carrying you to the car."

"Isn't it at the curb? There's no slush between here and there!"

"I'm just making sure you don't try to run off."

"Oh my God, put me down."

"Okay. Your feet are funny-looking." It's not true at all, but there's nothing about her that actually deserves a put-down.

She buries her face in my chest. "This is humiliating."

"No one will think any less of you just because you have the world's greatest boyfriend."

She laughs and covers her face with her hand.

"Now, darlin'. You really shouldn't be ashamed of having such a handsome, thoughtful, and hilarious boyfriend."

"You're killing me," she mumbles.

"How? By being such an amazing boyfriend? I'm going to keep saying it until it isn't weird for you that Keaton Bridges is your boyfriend. When do you think that will be?"

"Hmm. 2025 seems like a realistic goal."

"Aw, baby that's just foolish. By then you'll be well on your way to accepting the fact that I'm your amazing husband and the father of your children."

Manny holds the back door to my car open, and I place Roxy on the ground. She stares at me, mystified, shaking her head and pressing her lips together so tight, I know she's struggling to stop herself from responding with a snarky comeback. She swallows it down and kisses me on the cheek. "That dimple might kill me first. How have you managed to put up with this guy every day for so many years, Manny?"

"Well, miss," he says, "he pays me to."

"That makes sense."

We make out in the back seat all the way from New Jersey to Brooklyn. In between kisses, I ask her, "You want us to drop you off first?"

"No, I'll come with you to pick up Jackpot. But then I need to go home."

"You coming to my place tonight?"

Even as she's kissing me all over my face, she says, "No way. I need a night to myself. I'm gonna lie on my back and snore it up, and besides, we should take a little break from each other. See how we feel now that we're off the island."

"Fuck that. I'm taking you to dinner tomorrow."

"Okay," she says without even thinking about it. "But I get to choose where we go."

"In case you haven't noticed, *Ute*, that's what we've been doing all along."

Manny somehow manages to find a parking spot right in front of the dog hotel. I straighten myself up before stepping out of the car and try to sound casual when I ask Roxy, "You want to wait in the car?"

She smirks. "No. Why would you want me to wait in the car?"

I roll my eyes. "Can you do me a favor and wait in the car while I get him?"

"Because...?"

"Because I would like to give him the opportunity to get excited to see me."

"Sure. I will give *you* that opportunity."

"He does sometimes get happy to see me when I've been away for a few days."

"I have no doubt."

"This has been the longest period of time I've left him here, so it's important for us to re-establish the bond before—"

"Before he gets excited about bonding with someone he actually likes?"

I shake my head. "You're mean."

She pinches my cheek. "I hope he realizes how lucky he is to have such an amazing dog daddy. Maybe you should keep telling him you're his dog daddy until it doesn't feel weird to him."

That's not a bad idea, actually.

When I buzz the front door, the daytime manager lady smiles at me sympathetically when she lets me in. "Mr. Bridges. Welcome back—what a nice tan you have."

"Hi, thank you. Is he ready to go?"

"Oh yes, we have all of his things together, and he'll be so happy to see you." She pats me on the shoulder. "I'll call back to have someone bring him out."

"Great."

I sign for everything and try to shake off the nerves when the lady isn't looking. If I can win Foxy Roxy's heart, then I can win the love of a labradoodle, for Christ's sake. The door to the back rooms opens, and I'm so excited to see the little fucker, it's just stupid. "Hey, buddy! Hey, boy!"

He's wagging his tail, so cute and happy and energetic and then...he sees me, and he stands still and whimpers. He turns to jump up and paw at the closed door he just came out of.

"Look who it is, Jackpot! Look who it is, you good boy!" the guy who's holding on to his leash says. He tries to pull Jackpot toward me while reaching out to hand me my duffel bag with his belongings. Including the unwashed T-shirt of mine that I asked them to leave in his room so he'd remember how I smell. Well, that worked. Thanks, Internet.

"Jackpot!" I say, crouching down—because maybe if I'm more on his level, it'll be easier for him to realize how much he missed me. "C'mere, buddy!"

He whines and licks his chops, looks up at the guy and the lady, who both signal with their heads for him to go over to me. And he does. He trots on over to me and stands in front of me, staring just to the right of me while he lets me pet him. It's like when I was a kid and my mom was all, "Go give Aunt Bunny a hug!" and I'd trudge over and stand there to let my Great Aunt Bunny hug me while holding my breath so I didn't choke on the overwhelming scent of gin and vermouth, Parliament Lights, and Chanel No. 5.

But I'm feeling like the king of the world again. This counts as bonding. "He looks great!" I say. "Let's go home!"

My dog gives his friends one backward glance, sighs, and leads me to the door. He just wants to get this next part of his life over with, but I've got a trick up my sleeve, and I'm hoping it will score me some points with the asshole.

Sure enough, as soon as Roxy opens the car door, Jackpot is wagging his tail and jumping and barking a happy greeting. "Hey there, handsome! Get in here!" She pats her lap twice, and my dog springs up from the sidewalk right into her lap. I had no idea he could do that. Roxy gives him a thorough rubdown, and I'm not sure which one of them I'm more jealous of.

I shut the door and go around to the other side. I

guess I'm happy for them. He's giving my girlfriend's face a tongue bath when I get in. I drop the duffel bag on the floor between my legs. "I guess we go to Roxy's building now," I tell Manny. "Drive slow, for Jackpot's sake."

"Oh, you have such nice breath," she says to him. "Your fur smells so good too! Did they give him a bath?"

"Several."

"I wanna know what kind of shampoo they used, because it smells so good!" she says to Jackpot in a tone of voice she would never use with me.

"Roxpot foreva, I guess," I say under my breath.

Roxy hears me and pulls her head back, away from Jackpot's adoring tongue, trying to get him to turn around on her lap and face me. "Hey. Jackpot," she says authoritatively. "Sit here. Right here." She pats the seat between us. He steps off her lap and sits up straight exactly where she was pointing. "Good boy," she says, stroking him on the back of his neck. She motions for me to touch him.

We pet him, together, until we pull up in front of her building.

"You sure you don't want to spend the night with us?"

"Not tonight," she says as she leans across the dog to kiss me.

Manny parks and gets out to take her bags out of the trunk.

"Call me," I say.

"When?"

"As soon as you realize how much you miss me."

She scoffs at that. "I'll see you in just over twenty-four hours."

"And you're going to miss me the whole time. I want you to know that I won't judge you or think you're needy just because you call me in the middle of the night, wanting to hear my sexy reassuring voice. I'll be fine with that."

"Okay, pal. See you tomorrow." She gives Jackpot a kiss on the top of his head. I can tell he's getting anxious. "I will see you very soon," she says to him.

"Here," I say, pulling my unwashed Wharton T-shirt out of the duffel bag. "You can take this. It smells like me."

She laughs a lot harder than necessary because I'm only half joking. She does not take the T-shirt. "I'll text you later," she says, shaking her head.

"Yeah. You will."

As soon as Manny opens the door, Jackpot tries to bolt, but I'm holding on to his collar.

"Stay, Jackpot. You stay here with Keaton." She holds her finger up to him, and he barks out a complaint before sitting down again and staring up at her. "You need to be more forceful," she says to me.

"I'm coming back to pick you up at eight," I say to her —forcefully.

She giggles. "No. But that was good." She lets Manny help her out and doesn't say good-bye again or turn around.

And...Three. Two. One.

When she gets the front door unlocked, she looks over her shoulder and blows us a kiss before going inside.

Jackpot barks once.

"Yeah. She loves us. She'll be back."

CHAPTER 22
ROXY

Well, this is just dumb.

It's almost ten on a Thursday night and I'm not tired enough to sleep, but I don't want to be awake if I have to spend one more hour alone without Keaton fucking Bridges.

How did I go from being a reasonably sane and emotionally stable human being to being the woman who can't sleep in a bed unless Keaton is in it?

My skin hurts from going hours without being touched by him.

My lips don't know what to do anymore if they aren't kissing him.

My ears are straining to hear him say he's my boyfriend again.

I should have done laundry this evening, but I didn't want to wash his scent off my clothes. I should have just taken his stupid T-shirt. I should have just said he could come pick me up earlier. Now there's a freaking blizzard that's supposed to last a couple of hours, and I really need to sleep so I can be on my game when I go to work tomorrow.

I text Aimee to see if she's up. She isn't. Or if she is, she's doing all the things she needs to do before school and work tomorrow.

I can't believe Keaton hasn't texted me tonight. A couple of hours after they dropped me off, he sent me a picture of Jackpot, who was lying down in a dog bed and glancing up at the camera like—*what now, dude?* Keaton's caption was: **SO EXCITED TO BE HOME!!!**

I can't call him.

I scroll through my recent calls and texts to find someone else to call or text, but there's no one else I want to talk to or text more than The Man with No Socks, who has stealthily invaded my vagina and my heart.

I can't call him.

I am definitely not calling him.

I type out a text: **You up?**

Ten seconds later, I have a FaceTime call coming in from Keaton Bridges.

I accept the video call, and I am so happy to see his stupid handsome face, it's devastating.

"Are you in bed?" is the first thing he says.

"Yes, but I'm dressed and I'm *not* going to have Face-Time sex with you."

"Ever?"

"Tonight."

"Fair enough."

"What are you doing?"

He stretches his arms out in front of himself. He's at his computer and his hair is all mussed up, and I want to run my fingers through it and kiss his forehead. "I was just catching up on some work stuff. I should go to bed too, I'm beat. Hanging out with you for a week was exhausting."

I puff out a laugh. "Right back at you."

He grins. "How are you?"

"Awesome. Good. Okay. It was kind of weird coming home to an empty apartment. I was thinking about getting a pet, actually."

"You want mine?"

"Kind of."

"Because I can pretty much guarantee he wants you. Although I think he likes me more now because he can smell you on me."

Good. Excellent! I'm going to lay all of your clothes out on your bed and roll around on them so you can smell like me all day every day and everyone will know that you're mine.

"That's sweet. But we aren't allowed to have dogs in this building, remember? I could get a cat, though."

"Well, how's that going to play out when you move in with Jackpot and me?"

I drop my phone facedown on the duvet so he can't see me blushing and giggling like an idiot.

"I know you're smiling right now," I hear him say through the phone speaker. "You might as well let me see you."

I pick up the phone again and sigh. "I miss you."

"I miss you too."

"I hate being alone in bed now."

"Come over."

"There's a blizzard outside."

"I'll come over."

"No, you shouldn't leave Jackpot. Can we move dinner tomorrow up to lunch?"

"Fuck lunch. Let's meet somewhere for breakfast."

"The place I want to go to isn't open for breakfast."

"You would rather wait five extra hours to share a meal with me than eat at some other restaurant? We can do breakfast *and* lunch. And dinner. I'll reschedule everything and meet you anywhere."

"To be honest, I'm afraid I won't want to go to the office if I see you in the morning."

"Now that's more like it, *Ute*. It's on. Lunch tomorrow. Where are we going?"

"I will text you the location in the morning."

"I don't need to make a reservation?"

"I'll do it. One o'clock?"

"One o'clock."

"Wear socks."

"I'm only sockless when I wear loafers and flip-flops, asshat."

"Do you wear slippers at home?"

"Affirmative. I have two pairs of Brooks Brothers slippers—one for cold weather, one for warm—and I wear socks with neither of them."

I slap my forehead. How on earth did I end up with a hoity toity pretty boy who wears Brooks Brothers slippers? My dad would laugh so hard.

"Don't tell me I'm your first boyfriend to wear Brooks Brothers slippers." He smirks.

"I guess you're my first boyfriend who can afford slippers. Have you taught Jackpot to carry your slippers to you when you come home?"

"Sure. He brings me my slippers and the New York Times and then makes me an Old Fashioned and curls up at my feet while gazing up at me longingly."

"One day."

"Yes. One day."

I yawn. "Excuse me. I can't believe I'm yawning when this conversation is so stimulating."

"It's because you're no longer anxious now that you can see my face and hear my voice."

Oh my God, that is totally what it is.

"Or it's because..." Nope. I got nothing. My brain can't even come up with a snarky response. I'm broken. Keaton fucking Bridges has broken my brain. I sigh again —a defeated woman. "Yeah. That's what it is."

"Sweet dreams, *Ute*. I can't wait to see you tomorrow."

"I can't wait to see you either. Bye."

He waves, and I tap the red icon before I say something stupid like *I love you.*

I made sure to leave my office earlier than necessary before lunch because I want to be there to see Keaton's face when he walks into TGI Fridays for the first time in his life.

I wait near the hostess stand, facing the door and rubbing my hands together in anticipation.

I haven't been here in so long. This restaurant chain has a special place in my heart because when I was a kid, my dad would take my brother and me there to meet up with my mother after work, every other month. When I was twelve, it seemed like such a fun place to dine, and I imagined hanging out there with friends once I was in college. They served every kind of food that my brother and I wanted to eat and all the cocktails I couldn't wait to drink once I had a fake ID. When I was in college, Aimee officially became my BFF when she was the only person I knew there who would accompany me to the Ann Arbor location. Turned out TGI Fridays was not considered cool by many people over the age of fourteen in college towns—go figure. When she moved to Brooklyn, she became the only person who would ever join me at this location. I couldn't even get people to come ironically. I mean, I don't blame them—I wouldn't come here by myself. But it says "home" to me, and sometimes a girl needs a slider or four and a margarita or six. I haven't been able to get Aimee here since she had Finn, and it's probably just as well. Now that I'm in my thirties, I need to choose everything more wisely. Like appetizers and boyfriends.

I don't even realize how nervous I am about whether Keaton will actually show up or not, until he actually shows up. I see him step out of his car as Manny drops him off. He's wearing a charcoal gray wool overcoat and a long black scarf, and he looks so stylish and striking I actually catch my breath when he walks in.

"Mr. Bridges!" the hostess calls out before I can find my voice. "Nice to see you again!"

Keaton removes his gloves and holds his hand out to shake hers, nodding at everyone in the waiting area like he's entering a country club.

TGIWTF?

"My darling," he says to me, kissing me on the cheek and hugging me.

He smells so fucking good I want to bite his neck.

"You been waiting long?"

"Are you kidding me? You've been here before?"

His dimple pops out to make an unscheduled appearance. "Is that so surprising?"

I narrow my eyes at him. "I call bullshit."

"Okay, I came by when they opened and gave the hostess twenty bucks to greet me by name when I came back at lunch."

I punch his bicep, very meekly, because I'm laughing so hard. "You went to all that trouble in the middle of your first morning back to work?"

"Worth it." He claps his hands together once. "Let's do this!"

"Right this way, Mr. Bridges," the hostess says.

"She's on to us, Shari," he says. "You did great, though."

When Shari shows us to our table, he helps me off with my coat and then places it on the back of a chair for me. Wow. Nanny Rey did a really good job raising this one. When Shari hands him the menu, he looks at me and says, "I already know what I want. I checked out the menu online."

"I know what I want—I get the same thing every time."

Shari sends our waitress right over. I order the spinach & artichoke dip, a bacon cheeseburger, and a margarita.

"That's my girl," he says. "I would like to try your mozzarella sticks, the filet mignon, medium-rare, topped with whiskey glaze, an Oreo Madness to share for dessert, and—what do you recommend as a cocktail pairing, Rachel? What's your favorite?" he asks the waitress.

"I mean, you can't go wrong with the Ultimate Long Island Tea."

"That's what I'm talking about, Rachel! One of those for me, and you know what? I'd like to order a round of drinks for all the other guests here today!" he says very loudly. "It's Friday, and we're celebrating!"

The table full of office workers next to us cheers.

"TGI Fridays!" he says, raising his hands in the air.

"You're insane," I say, covering my face. "What are you celebrating?"

"Us, dummy." He takes my hand from my face and kisses it. "We're celebrating us." He holds his phone up and leans in closer to me. "Stop looking all misty-eyed and smile. You need to send a picture of us to your parents."

When he was halfway done with his Ultimate Long Island Tea, Keaton decided to send the picture of us at TGI Fridays to his parents too.

He said that a few hours later, his mother wrote back:

What fun! You look very tan and fit. Dad agrees. The girl is very pretty.

Our friends' responses on our group text were somewhat more amusing.

AIMEE MCKAY: Aww. You guys are adorable, and I miss that place. Say hi to the margaritas for me.

CHASE MCKAY: Did she kidnap you, Bridges? Is this a cry for help?

NINA DEVLIN: I am so jealous of your tans. And how cute you guys are. And that you're getting drunk while I teach kids about fractions.

VINCE DEVLIN: Hey Rox, when he agreed to meet you there, did you explain to him that a slider was an appetizer and not a sex thing?

BERNADETTE FARMER: Can you guys bring me a bucket of ribs? I'm starving.

BERNADETTE FARMER: Also #ROXTON4EVA

MATT MCGOVERN: <neutral face emoji>

MATT MCGOVERN: Also #ROXTON4EVA

Keaton was so upbeat and polite while we were at the restaurant, but I could tell he didn't really like the food and that he didn't feel great once we were finally done eating and drinking. His delicate little rich boy's digestive system isn't used to handling so many calories and so much saturated fat all at once. Instead of letting him take me to SoHo for dinner like he was planning to, I insisted on bringing him peppermint tea and the ingredients for a chicken and rice soup that my mom always makes when a loved one has an upset tummy.

I was not prepared for how freaking gorgeous and huge his townhouse is.

Keaton was not prepared for how freaking delicious my homemade soup is.

Neither of us were prepared for how enthusiastically and relentlessly Jackpot would hump my freaking leg. He is neutered, but Keaton thinks it's the cocoa butter lotion I've been using. I just don't want to stop using it because it reminds me of the vacation. But the skin on my shin actually started to chafe. The door to the bedroom is closed, and we try to ignore the dog, who is scratching at and around outside it.

"I feel so much closer to Jackpot now," Keaton says as he peels off my cardigan and kisses my shoulder and my neck before pulling off my camisole. "We finally have something in common."

"An aversion to shitting in the snow?" I have to place my hands on his chest to keep from swaying. His kisses still feel new and unnerving in the best way.

"Good point. We now have two things in common. That and an irresistible desire to mount you and claim you for our own."

"I appreciate that you yourself haven't made me chafe yet."

"Yet." He traces along the scalloped edge of my bra with his fingertip and then unhooks it at the back. I watch his face as he watches my breasts spill out and into the palms of his confident hands. There's a reverence in his expression that humbles me while also making me feel so much more than foxy. I feel like a queen.

In many ways we're so familiar to each other, but the sense of discovery is still thrilling, and I hope it lasts. I hope all of it lasts. I've even started to imagine what he'd look like as he gets older, and I want to be here to watch him become a silver fox. I had my career mapped out before I graduated from high school, but this is the first time I've really thought about what the future would look like with a man, beyond a few years at a time.

In just a few days, I've gone from being shocked that he could be The One to being shocked that I had spent so long convincing myself that he couldn't be.

I undress him just as slowly and attentively as he undressed me, paying special attention to his chest—the one that I now absolutely believe most women can't handle seeing. It is perfect. His pecs are beautifully formed and covered with a sparse layer of light-brown hair that gradually became more golden in the sun, and I can't keep my hands or my lips off it.

"Fucking hell," he says in a totally different tone from how he usually says those two words when we're getting naked with each other. "I'm sorry. I have to put him in his room."

"Yeah, that's getting hard to ignore." Jackpot has been whining and whimpering and rattling the door.

"You might want to hide in the bathroom before I open this door."

I do.

By the time Keaton returns, I am in his bed, completely naked between the most luxurious sheets I have ever luxuriated in. The big, sturdy, and reliable bed frame and the heavy masculine headboard with these billion thread count sheets is a heady combination that sends all the blood straight to my lady parts in the same way that his refined but fearless hands do.

"Well now. Don't you look right at home in my bed."

"What kind of sheets are these?"

"Magical. Because they're mine." He drops his pants and boxers to the floor and climbs in with me.

We both groan because the feel of skin on skin and skin on sheets is so exquisite. The weight of his body on mine is what I've been missing since last night. That's a lie, I've missed every single thing about him, everything he says, everything he does to me.

My hands are roaming all over his back when he hikes my legs up and pushes inside me. I've been wet for him since last night—since last week, really—and everything about the way we are together now is smooth with just a hint of the friction we used to have, and it is delicious and wonderful.

"Fuck, I've missed being inside you," he mutters. "I don't know how I made it through the day."

"Make up for last night," I say. "Make up for all the lost time. Don't hold back. Just break the fucking bed if you can."

I hear air blow out of his nostrils, and he says, as he

presses down into his hands to raise his torso up, "This bed was custom-made, and I said to the guys who installed it that I wanted it to withstand King Kong-style jungle sex. But you're the only woman I've ever been with who's asked for it."

"I'm not asking."

"Fucking hell, you are my kind of lady." His thrusts come at me slow and strong and then hard and fast.

He wasn't kidding about this bed; it isn't moving, even though I am pretty sure if it weren't for the two pillows behind my head, I'd have a concussion already.

He grabs hold of the top of the headboard for leverage, and I grip the sides of the pillow, both of us panting and crying out.

I've never wanted so badly to feel like someone's becoming a part of me.

I want to feel him between my legs all day tomorrow —or for the rest of my life, maybe.

This orgasm is a jolt to the system. It shakes me to my core and shatters my soul and reassembles me into a person who can tell this man exactly what I'm feeling. Or I wish it would, anyway.

When he comes, he makes a sound that's so masculine and primal and vulnerable, I hold on to him tight, soothing him so he knows I'm here with him, taking all of him into me.

He collapses onto me so beautifully, slick with sweat, warm, and emptied out.

I can feel his heart pounding against my chest.

I know we're both thinking the same thing. It's in the silence and the way we run our fingers through each other's hair so tenderly but possessively. It's in our labored breaths and the air around us. Maybe there's some untranslatable word—Japanese or Swahili—that means all the things I'm feeling for him and I just haven't learned it yet. I'll find it. I'll find some perfect thing to say to him that I've never said to anyone else before. He deserves it.

"I didn't even come close to breaking this bed" is what he finally says when he catches his breath.

"You will. You'll wear it down eventually. I have no doubt."

CHAPTER 23
KEATON

Roxy Carter and I have spent the last ten nights in a row together, in the same bed.

We still haven't broken mine, but it's not for lack of trying. Apparently the only thing stronger than my primal drive to screw the living daylights out of my very willing hot girlfriend is walnut wood, bed bolts, and expertly crafted mortise and tenon joint connections. Interestingly, she wanted me to go easy on her when we stayed at her place.

It has been fun and blissful, despite that awkward falling-in-love problem of deciding when to say "I love you" for the first time. *Not* saying it right before coming has become the best kind of daily struggle. We still banter and talk like friends, but the quiet moments between us echo with unspoken words.

Incidentally, there *is* a word for what's happening, courtesy of the indigenous people of Tierra del Fuego. I can never remember how to spell it and I have no idea how to pronounce it, but it's a single word that describes the wordless, meaningful look between two people who both have a desire to initiate something but they're both reluctant to start. It's a beautiful and fragile time, not bad at all, and I have savored it.

But I have to leave for a three-day business trip tomorrow morning, so I'm planning on telling her tonight when we see each other.

My ex-girlfriend Tamara has been texting me every day for the past week, telling me that she's moved back and asking to see me. I kept telling her I was busy—and I am—but I can't put it off any longer. I don't particularly want to see her, but there's something I've wanted to ask her for years, and besides...I don't want her showing up unannounced when Roxy's with me. I agreed to meet her for coffee at a place near my office in DUMBO.

I text Roxy while I'm waiting outside the café, telling her that Jackpot and I can't wait to see her tonight. I not only smile whenever I receive a text from her, I smile when I write to her. I'm fucking adorable. As soon as I've sent it, I look up and see a ghost crossing the street toward me. Not of the demon variety, but one who haunted me gently and tenaciously for a lot longer than she should have.

Tamara is about five years older since I last saw her, I guess. She doesn't walk as quickly as a native Manhattanite anymore, and she's adopted a more casual West Coast style, but she's still as put-together as ever. I suppose, if things were different right now, she'd still turn my head. But she doesn't. Or rather, I turn my head to look around the area to make sure Roxy isn't there. It's not that I feel guilty. I just don't want any misunderstandings now that things are going so well for us.

Tamara flings her arms around me without hesitation —another sign she's adapted to the LA lifestyle. "Oh my God, it's good to see you."

I pat her on the back and pull away. "Hey, you. Welcome back."

"I am *so* glad to be back—you have no idea. Have you been waiting long? I'm not late, am I? I'm not used to walking everywhere yet."

"Just got here. Shall we?" I open the door to the café.

She touches my waist as she passes through the door. I used to love how relatively touchy-feely she was for a New Yorker, but now it just seems presumptuous.

The only free table is by the window, and I don't realize until after I've sat down that Tamara was waiting for me to pull her chair out for her. I always used to. She doesn't make a fuss about it, though. She wouldn't. That's why I liked her. Low drama.

We don't say anything to each other until after ordering coffee from the waitress.

"You look really good, Keaton," she says, leaning forward, like she's confiding in me.

"Thank you. I just got back from vacation."

"Really? Where'd you go?"

"Antigua."

"I'd love to go there! We had such a good time at St. Barts. I still think about that vacation a lot."

Yeah. I should have known that from all the nothing you wrote in your annual e-cards.

"So what's up? I saw your brother at the airport a couple of weeks ago. I don't know if he mentioned it."

"Really? No, he didn't tell me that—you know how he is. So you knew that I was moving back? He told you?"

"Yes."

"Oh. I'm sorry." She reaches across the small table to touch my hand. "Moving was so crazy, I didn't have time to get in touch with people."

I pull my hand away to pick up a sugar packet that I won't be using for the coffee that hasn't been brought to me yet. "It's not a problem, I totally get it. What's up? I have another meeting in less than half an hour, so..."

"Right. So..." She waits until the waitress finishes placing our coffees in front of us. "So, I wanted to talk to you because I was hoping you would give me some business advice. I'm setting up a new company—publicity for feature-length documentaries.

"Cool."

"Yeah, that kind of became my thing out in LA, when I was doing publicity for finance companies. But I'm branching out on my own and looking at office space and meeting with potential new hires. It's just so overwhelming, and I still need to write up a business plan and all that stuff, and I mean...you have the best head for business of anyone I know, so..." She rests her hand on top of my forearm. "Can I borrow your brain?"

I reach for a napkin that I don't need so I can move my arm away. "I appreciate the compliment, but to be honest, I think it would be better if I ask Chase if you can call him for advice. He's the one who's actually founded two startups. I'm just the money guy.

"Oh." She looks down. "Yeah, that makes sense. Thanks."

"Also, I have a girlfriend now, so it wouldn't be a good idea for me to be in touch with you. It's still new. Kind of."

"Oh. Good. Who is it?" She says it like she wants to know which socialite I'm dating this time.

"Roxy."

She snorts laughs and then checks my expression to see if I'm being serious. "*Roxy* Roxy? Like, Foxy Roxy?"

"I'm well aware of the incongruities, but yes. *The* Foxy Roxy."

"Wow. I guess that's not so surprising, really."

"It's not?"

"Well..." She twists her lips to the side, sheepishly. "I was always a little jealous of her, if you must know."

"You were? I had no idea."

"Yeah. Well. I'm a good little East Coast WASP." She nods her head once, as if she's made a decision. "I'm happy for you."

"Thanks. Me too. Are you? Seeing anyone?"

"No. I mean, there was someone in LA, but it didn't make sense once I'd decided to move back here."

"Right. Why would it?" I say, surprised by how bitter that sounded.

She stares down at her untouched cup of coffee and straightens herself up. "Well, I guess we both have other places to get to..."

"Can I ask you one thing?"

She continues to stare at the coffee cup. "Why didn't I want you to move to LA with me?"

She always did know what was on my mind, even if she didn't always tell me what I needed to hear.

"Yeah. I mean, I'm glad I didn't, obviously. But I wondered for a long time."

She leans back in her chair and looks down at her hands, which are in her lap. "I did love you, Keaton. You were good to me. But I never felt like I was the most important person to you."

I can't help but laugh at that. "I was willing to drop everything and move across the country to be with you."

"I know, I know. But I saw how you were with your friends. You were always so much happier and funnier with them. You'd do anything for them. I know you offered to come to LA with me, but I don't think you truly *wanted* to." She pauses for me to respond.

I don't, because she's right. I wanted to be with her, I wanted her to want to be with me, but of course I didn't want to leave my friends and my job and move to LA.

She finally looks up at me, her voice quivering just a little. "It makes sense that you'd end up with Roxy. I mean, it doesn't make sense at all, but you know what I mean."

I smile at that. "Yeah. I do."

When she gets up to leave, I hug her and say good-bye in the way that I wasn't able to before. Not *good-bye for now until you realize what a huge mistake you're making*. Not *good-bye, fuck you, you never deserved me anyway, good luck over there on the* Worst Coast *of America*. A real *good-bye, I don't expect to see you again, but thank you*.

As soon as she's out the door, I signal to the waitress

for the check and then I check my phone for a reply from Roxy, but there isn't one. Which is weird because she's a compulsive responder. Whether we're talking or texting or just raising our eyebrows at each other, she's the comeback queen. Even when she's in a meeting, she usually replies within ten minutes—she works at an online retail company, not a hospital.

I write another message, and for the first time since before we left for Antigua, I'm not smiling like an idiot.

ME: We still on for dinner tonight?

The animated dots come up almost immediately, which means she probably saw my earlier text and didn't respond.

UTE: I'm so sorry, Keaton. I won't be able to make it tonight. Something just came up, and I have to deal with it.

Okay, that's troubling. She never calls me by my first name in texts, and since when does she say things like "I'm so sorry." Maybe someone stole her phone.

ME: If this is really you, tell me where I have a birthmark or send me a boob pic.

ME: Never mind. Just send a new boob pic. Of your boobs.

UTE: It's me, dummy. Sometimes I write weird things like sorry. Or Keaton.

ME: So that's a no re. the boob pic?

UTE: It's a not now. Please refer to your ever-growing library of them for the moment.

ME: You better send me at least one a day for the next three days, then. I expect a minimum of six boobs to add to my library.

I get no response to that.

ME: Are you saying you can't make it to dinner or that you aren't spending the night either?

UTE: Can't do either. Sorry. I'll miss you. Have a good trip. See you when you get back. Please tell me you aren't one of those giant pussies who wants me to pick you up at the airport.

ME: Please tell me you aren't one of those giant pussies who wants to pick me up at the airport.

UTE: I would sooner pick up trash along the freeway.

ME: We're so perfect for each other.

UTE: You're going to Finn's party on Saturday, right?

ME: I will rock that house party. Thanks for reminding me to order birthday presents.

UTE: Don't worry. The good godparent has it covered.

ME: Dream on. I'll miss you.

Fucking hell, I want to tell her I love her, but she'd dropkick me if I do it in a text for the first time. There's no sign of another text from her, and I guess she already told me she'll miss me, so I put my phone away, pay the bill, and head back to my office. The smile's still on my face when my meeting starts, but some strange, unsettling feeling lingers. I'm certain that it's just from seeing a significant ex and knowing that I want Tamara to be the last ex-girlfriend I ever have.

CHAPTER 24
ROXY

id you do it yet? Aimee mouths to me as soon as I open the door. I nod at her and then look down at Finn, who's standing right in front of her, clutching his iPad case and standing remarkably still as he waits for me to invite him into my apartment.

"Hey, buddy!" I say, bending down and holding my hand out for him to slap it.

"Hey," he mumbles. He tucks the iPad case under one arm and slaps me five and then very half-heartedly participates in the super special handshake we made up a few months ago. The handshake involves fist bumping, butt shaking, and turning around while flapping our arms like a chicken, and then it ends with us making a fart noise with our tongues. It feels a lot less awesome when he isn't into it.

"Well, thanks for coming over, you guys. Come on in." I watch Finn let his little backpack fall from his slouched shoulders and then to the floor as he trudges over to my sofa.

"Hey. Pick that up, mister!" Aimee says.

"Ugh. Where am I supposed to put it?" he moans.

"I'll just put it by the door here," I say, picking it up for him. "What crawled up his bum?" I ask his mother.

"He just found out that his best friend has to visit his grandparents out of town this weekend, so he'll miss the party."

"Awww, that's a bummer, Finn! But hey—I'll be there!"

"Thanks," he says, all mopey. "Can I watch Netflix?" he asks both of us.

"Absolutely," I say. "Your mom and I are just gonna go in the kitchen to get us snacks. Oh—but don't go into the bathroom for a while, okay?"

"Why? Does it smell?"

"Yeah. Sure."

Aimee drops all of her bags near the door and follows me to the kitchen. There's no door, so we talk quietly— not that Finn has any interest in anything other than *Cloudy with a Chance of Meatballs* and his own misery.

I flick my hands, in an attempt to release the anxiety I've been trying to harness in front of my godson, because it is vitally important that he thinks of me as cool at all times. But my heart is racing, my armpits are damp, and I have felt on the verge of tears all day.

"Keaton should be here with you," Aimee says, rubbing my back. "Or you should at least be talking to him. You're really not going to call him?"

"I need to know what to say to him first, and he's going out of town for a few days. I don't want him thinking about this while he's dealing with this new investment thing."

"Okay. Are you okay?"

"Do I look okay?"

"No." She opens the fridge to pull out the organic string cheese packets that I keep stocked in case of a Finn visit. "You look like a spaz. I'm glad you called me."

"I don't know why I'm so nervous. It's so dumb. I've done this before. Like, twice, and it's always a false alarm."

She nudges the fridge door closed and gives me a look. "Do you really not know why you're nervous?"

I cover my face. "I literally didn't know it was possible for me to get nervous until this morning... Hey, how old is Tamara now? Late twenties?"

"His ex? Why are you even thinking about that right now?"

"Just tell me so I can stop wondering."

"I mean...I guess she'd be twenty-eight."

I swallow hard. "Right."

"And that is irrelevant."

"I know."

"*Do* you?"

"Nope! Fuck, I miss being twenty-eight. Being almost thirty-five sucks all the donkey balls."

She puts the cheese down on the counter and crosses her arms in front of her chest. I am entirely sure that she is loving this—being the calm, rational one in our relationship, after all my years of unsolicited advice-giving wiseassery whenever she found herself in a dating situation that just made me laugh.

God, I miss those days.

Or do I?

Is part of me loving this angsty little minidrama that's playing out in my brain too? Because it has been so long since I felt anything even remotely like this, anything even remotely this much. Because of *Keaton fucking Bridges.*

"Roxy. What are you hoping the result will be?"

I take a deep, shaky breath before answering, because I haven't really even allowed myself to form this thought in my head until now. "A plus sign. I wasn't planning for it and it's way too soon, but for the first time ever, I wouldn't mind if it's a plus sign." And that's when I finally let myself cry. For the first time since Finn was born, I cry like a big baby.

Aimee has wrapped me in her arms, and I just hang there like I ragdoll.

When I got to work this morning and looked at my calendar, I'd realized that it was time to start a new pack of birth control pills, and that was also when I'd realized that I never got a period. I'd been so caught up in being with Keaton that I lost track of pretty much anything that wasn't scheduled into my calendar or right in front of me. It doesn't even make sense that I'd get pregnant because I never missed a pill, but with the traveling and everything...I haven't been taking it every twenty-four hours for the past few weeks. You never know. Knowing Keaton, he probably has exceptionally persistent and charming sperm. They'd be all: "All right, egg, here's how it's going down. I'm going to penetrate you, and you're going to love it, and I'm just gonna wait here until it happens. And it. Will. Happen."

"I want you to get what you want, Rox, but I'm just going to say that even if you don't get a plus sign this time, that doesn't mean you won't another time."

"I know, I know. But he wants a bunch of kids, and how the hell is he going to do that if he's with me? I would have to have a baby every year. I'd have to quit my job."

"Well, now you're getting way ahead of yourself."

"I just want to give him what he wants," I sob into her neck. "What if I can't?"

"You haven't asked him if *not* having a bunch of kids is a deal breaker for him, though, have you?"

I snort. "If I ever have that kind of conversation with anyone, please shoot me."

"Roxanne. You are in a serious adult relationship with Keaton. That's the kind of conversation that serious adults who are in relationships have when they're almost thirty-five."

"Ugh." I pull away from her, wipe my eyes, and slouch my shoulders while moaning just like Finn did. "But we haven't had enough fun yet."

She hands me a paper towel. "Oh really? That's not what it sounded like on Valentine's Day when you were screaming so loud you woke up the whole island."

I laugh so hard while blowing my nose, I think some of my mushy brain came shooting out. "You heard that?"

"I'm pretty sure everyone in the Caribbean heard it."

Thinking of that shower at the resort reminds me of what's waiting for me on my bathroom counter. "Shit. It's been way longer than five minutes since I peed on it. I'll have to do it again."

"Do you have another one?"

"I bought five boxes."

"Atta girl. Want me to come with you?"

I shake my head. "But don't leave until I come out, okay?"

"Please. I'll be right here until you kick us out. And remember it'll be fine either way."

My hand is trembling as I reach for the doorknob to my bathroom. I don't know why I've gotten so worked up and convinced myself that the future of my relationship with Keaton depends on what a plastic stick tells me today. I just know that I want Keaton, and I want Keaton to have what he wants, and I want him to want me, but I don't know if I can give him everything that he wants and deserves, and that feels terrible.

I inhale, slow and deep, remembering the Zoltar Speaks card that Chase gave me. Winds of change. Soon everything will come down to a better order. It'll be fine. Plus or minus. Now or later. Me and Keaton. I open the door and look right at the plastic stick on the counter.

It'll be fine.

CHAPTER 25
KEATON

Text messaging is an interesting way to connect with a person. I can remember a time in my life —about four days ago—when I would always smile while writing and reading text messages to and from one Miss Roxanne Carter. I'd send her a message. She'd respond by writing a message back to me. Sometimes, if I was lucky, she'd respond by sending a picture instead of a string of snappy words. It was fun. It was even a little bit thrilling. It was one of the many different ways we connected with each other. It wasn't my favorite, but it was in the top ten for sure.

Now all of a sudden, it's the only way she'll communicate with me.

I call her, it goes to voice mail. I FaceTime her, she doesn't accept the call. She always responds with a text saying she's so sorry she missed my call. What was I calling about?

Well, I was hoping I could actually speak to her on the phone to tell her what I was calling about, because I was calling about wanting to talk to her and hear her voice. Being able to see her at the same time would be an added bonus and something that is technologically possible in these exciting times that we now live in—so why not? Especially when we're in different cities. Especially because we're dating. Especially because we both supposedly miss each other.

Roxy fucking Carter has found a whole new way to drive me crazy, and she's doing it in the last way I ever would have imagined possible—by *not* talking back to me.

How did we go from spending every night together and staying in touch all day long to only texting back and forth a few times a day—for more than three days?

I called Chase to ask if he'd seen or talked to her. "No, but Aimee and Finn were at her place a few days ago before dinner."

"So she's okay?"

"Sure. I mean, Aimee didn't say anything, so I think we can assume she's okay."

I told him she wasn't calling me back, just texting. He said she's "probably just being Roxy." Which made a lot of sense when he said it, but I don't even know what that means anymore. Which Roxy is she being? Did she revert back to the post-wedding Foxy Roxy who can't deal with how awesome we were together? Or is this how Roxy is when she suddenly decides she doesn't want to date the awesome guy she's awesome with? There are a million reasons for not calling a person back, and none of them are good.

I kept looking around when I was at the airport, thinking that maybe this was all leading up to a big surprise—that she'd be there at Arrivals waiting for me, in heels and a chauffeur's cap, a *Mr. Bridges* sign, and in a trench coat with nothing on underneath. She wasn't. I feel bad about looking so disappointed when I only saw Manny there to greet me that I'll probably have to give him another raise.

When I picked up Jackpot at the dog hotel, he was so excited to see me. But when we got to the car and there was no Roxy in the back seat, he looked back at me, sighed, and frowned. *You blew it with her, didn't you?* he was thinking.

Did I? Did she see me with Tamara? Is that what this is? Is she the kind of woman who would show up to surprise me at work and then not tell me that she saw me with my ex-girlfriend and then be passive-aggressive about it? I don't think so, but I've been wrong about women once or fifty times before.

I've re-read her messages over and over, and they aren't passive-aggressive or curt or incendiary. They're just brief and to the point. *We'll talk at Finn's party* is what she keeps telling me. She just doesn't want to talk to me until then for some reason. Even now that I'm back at home.

It's one thing to be shut out of a couples vacation when you're not part of a couple, but being shut out of being a couple just hurts.

If that's what this is.

She texted that she'll be helping Chase and Aimee set up for the party tomorrow morning, so I call Aimee before she goes to bed.

"Keaton?"

"What the hell is going on?"

"Um, what is this regarding?"

"Why won't she talk to me?"

"Oh…" I can hear her exhale for five terrible seconds before continuing. "She's fine. You're fine. I wish I could say something to calm you down, but I can't be the one who explains it to you. I'm sorry."

"There's an 'it'?"

"Things. I can't be the one who explains things to you. You're coming to the party, right? Everyone's gonna be here. After naptime. Two-ish?"

"I'll be there after my nap. Will she?"

"Of course she will. Just hang in there. You guys just need to talk in person. I gotta go, but it'll be fine."

Maybe I really am overreacting.

I dig up my old notebook from college, the one with all the untranslatable words in it, and flip through looking for something that describes all these new anxious feelings I'm having.

Nope.

Shitty will have to suffice.

Confused.

Lovesick.

I just refuse to add another thing to that list: *dumped.*

I get into bed, punch the pillow, and settle in for a long, sleepless night. No use even trying to stay awake if I can't see or talk to Roxy. I'm not even in the mood to angrily jerk off to memories of Bikini Roxy or Shower Roxy—that's how bad it is. I just miss *my* Roxy. I miss Ute.

After about ten minutes of lying here, stewing, I feel another new thing.

The weight of a dog jumping up onto the bed.

I might be imagining it, but I don't want to move to look and risk startling him. I can hear Jackpot sniffing around, exploring the side of the bed that I'm not on. I can tell from the jingling of his collar tags that he's circling in on the area by the pillow that Roxy usually sleeps on. Finally, he plops down with a little groan.

After he's still for a few minutes, I slowly turn to get a look. Jackpot's chin is resting on the pillow, and his back is to me, and I know this is all about him missing Roxy, but I count this as a win. Always one to push my luck, I reach over to stroke the fur on the back of his neck. He lets me. It's the best thing that's happened to me in the past few days. Closing a deal with a hot startup in Toronto was nothing compared to this.

I'm the king of the fucking world again, and tomorrow I'll be bringing my queen back home for both of us.

CHAPTER 26
ROXY

'm looking around at twelve adorable, happy, hyper kids, and I'm exhausted, even though I'll only have to be around them for a couple of hours.

This party is a monster bash. I've been here since this morning, helping Aimee decorate and hide cute little monster dolls around the living room area for a treasure hunt while Chase kept Finn busy at an early matinee. Now Finn has had his nap, and he's done moping about his best friend's absence. Matt and Bernadette and Vince and Nina are here with Harriet and Joni. Tiny party guests have been dropped off for the past fifteen minutes. The photo booth has been delivered and set up, the face painter lady is here, the balloon guy has arrived, but Keaton fucking Bridges is not in the building.

Figures.

It's the first time I've ever *wanted* to see him at one of these gatherings, and he doesn't show up when he's expected to.

I have been so impatiently waiting to talk to him in

person and completely unable to risk chatting with him in any other way because I need this to come out just right.

I run to the kitchen to get a roll of paper towels when I spot a little girl who spilled her cup of fruit punch on the floor after a boy knocked her arm while pushing past her. She is looking around, not knowing what to do and trying so hard not to cry when I get to her. I kneel down on the floor and wipe up the little fuchsia-pink puddle.

"Hey, sweetie. I got this. Don't worry."

"I'm sorry. It was an accident."

"I know. I saw what happened. It definitely wasn't your fault."

"Ethan should be the one who cleans it up."

"You're right. When you grow up, just remember that if a boy makes a mess and tries to clean it up himself, then he's a boy worth hanging on to."

She wrinkles her little nose. "I don't want to hang on to a boy."

"Or a girl. Or no one. You don't have to hang on to anyone. Nobody does! But I tell you what—it's not a sign of weakness if you do. Remember that."

She looks at me like I'm weird, and I guess I am, and I don't blame her for walking off.

When I stand up to throw the paper towels away, I see that Keaton has arrived and he's placing a huge, professionally wrapped gift on the gift table while chatting with Chase and Matt and Vince.

He looks tired, and it makes him even more boyishly handsome than usual. Irresistible. To me, anyway. Like the grown-up version of the little boy who missed his nanny Reyna. The hesitant expression that settles on his face when we lock eyes rips my heart in two.

I can't even move. I just stand here, watching him walk toward me. "Hi," he says, putting his hand on my arm and leading me away from the living room area. "Can I talk to you alone for a second?"

"Yes."

This place is a loft, so the only rooms that have doors are the bathrooms and bedrooms. He pulls me into the guest bedroom/office and shuts the door. I expect him to grab me and kiss me, but instead he crosses his arms in front of his chest and says, "I don't know what's going on with you, but whatever it is—it ends now. In case it is what I'm afraid it is, I will tell you this—Tamara was texting and asking to see me last week, but I kept putting it off because I didn't want to see her and I wanted to spend all of my available time with you. That day before I left town, I met with her for like ten minutes by my office, in which time I learned that she wanted to pick my brain about business matters and I immediately told her that it would be better for her to talk to Chase about that stuff because I have a girlfriend. That was it. That was the last time I'll ever see or talk to her, as far as I'm concerned." His warm brown eyes scan my face for a reaction.

I'm still processing what he's telling me, but it seems to me that if that's true, then he dealt with it perfectly. And that is so annoying. "Okay... That's interesting. I'm not sure what to say."

"Well, I would personally love it if you'd tell me how you feel about what I just told you. Let's start with that."

"All right." I cross my arms, mimicking him. Like we're having some sort of negotiation. This is not how I had planned for our talk to go. "I suppose I'm a little surprised that I didn't know you saw Tamara. But I also don't need to know your whereabouts at all times, and I appreciate that you told her about me."

He sighs, closes his eyes, and pinches the bridge of his nose with his fingers. "I was going to tell you about it when I saw you that night. So what you're saying is, you didn't see us together?"

"Why would I have seen you? Were you worried that I had seen you? Was there a reason you wouldn't have wanted me to see you with her? Hang on. Are you telling me everything?"

He scrubs his face with the palm of his hand. He does this a lot when he's with me. "I will always tell you everything you want to know and then some—I'm just trying to figure out what's going on, Roxy. So that's not what you're being weird about?"

"No."

Look at this boy, trying to clean up a little mess that he thought he made. I need to hang on to him.

"It would be fantastic if you could tell me exactly why you stopped taking and returning my calls all of a sudden, because you're ruining my life."

"I told you I would talk to you here. Today."

"Well, here we are—today! Talk to me. I need to know what the problem is so I can fix it."

"I have a whole thing planned—geez."

"Do you have a Power Point presentation to set up? Just start talking."

"Not. Here." This man is infuriating, and my clitoris is about to detonate.

He's standing in front of the door, bigger than ever and belligerent. When I try to nudge him out of the way, that's when he finally grabs my shoulders, presses me up against the door, and kisses me. Thank God. This is all I've wanted since the second I saw him. I inhale the delicious scent of him. I have been craving it for days. My hands are immediately on his face, and his hands slide down to my waist, but my mouth and tongue and teeth are basically having an argument with his mouth and tongue and teeth, and it's everything that I need right now but also not nearly enough.

"You're driving me crazy," he mutters.

"I wasn't trying to."

"You're a fucking pain in my ass, you know that?"

"Don't swear around the kids."

He kisses me on that spot, that spot on my neck, and my knees go weak. "If they can hear us in here, we're already in trouble."

"I've missed you so much," I whimper. I've lost the ability to hold my head up.

"You should have called me."

"I couldn't say the things I have to say to you on the phone."

"Just tell me now. Tell me everything, you wretched woman." He kisses along my jaw and then my mouth.

I mean...would it be the worst thing in the world if we had a quickie in here while a bunch of young children and our closest friends get their faces painted down the hall?

I turn my head to the side and duck out of the way, and it's painful to move away from those lips and those hands, but I have to do this. We need to get out of here before I try to engulf him with my vulva. "Come with me," I say as I drag my fingers through my hair and straighten out my sweater. I glance down at his semi. "Put that thing away."

"Great fucking idea waiting until a child's birthday party to see me for the first time in days," he grumbles while readjusting himself.

"Excuse me for thinking you could keep your hands to yourself."

He shakes his head and reaches for the doorknob. "Piece of work." He slaps me on the behind and opens the door. "Get out."

We remind me of my parents all of a sudden. I love our dynamic, but I know we still aren't out of the woods yet. I still need to have an actual grown-up relationship talk with him, and it could still ruin everything.

"Wait for me here," I say to him.

He rolls his eyes and stands in the living room, watching the kids get their faces painted like *Monsters, Inc* characters while the *Trolls* soundtrack plays at a respectable volume from the house speakers. I go to the kitchen to grab two bottles of the Blue Moon beer that I brought this morning. When I come out again, I nod for him to follow me. There is just enough controlled chaos in here that we can slip out for a while unnoticed.

"Come outside with me." I hold both bottles by their necks in one hand and lead him to the back patio with the other. We're both wearing sweaters and it is not quite cold enough to have to put on a coat. It's not exactly warm out, but it is sunny, and the snow has melted.

"Where are we going?" he grumbles.

"Here. Look, dummy," I say, tilting my chin up at the sky. "It's the first sunny day after a long winter." I hand him an open bottle and sit down on one of the patio chairs, gesturing for him to take a seat in the other. "It's not warm, but we're going to have a beer outside."

He sits down, grinning. *"Utepils."* He's getting it now. He scoots his chair closer to mine so we're knee to knee.

I look right at him, taking a deep breath before launching into it. "I've been trying so hard to find some perfect, dazzling thing to say to you. I don't know how you suddenly managed to start saying the exact right thing to me at the right time a few weeks ago, but you make it seem easy. And it isn't. It's really hard. I didn't find a word. I don't have the words. I don't know how to say what you mean to me. In any language." I shrug and clink my beer bottle with his. "I love you. So much. I'm so in love with you. I'm sorry I haven't said it before, but I promise I'll never stop saying it if you stick with me."

He inhales and opens his mouth, but I cover it with my hand.

"Let me get all of this out first." I wait for him to nod in agreement before moving my hand away, sighing.

"I thought I was pregnant. For like, a day. Long story short—I'm on the pill, as you know—but I didn't get a period. And I also didn't get a plus sign on the pee stick. But for the first time ever, I wasn't afraid of a plus sign. I went to the gynecologist and they did an ultrasound, just to be safe once we knew I wasn't pregnant, but the doctor said sometimes you just don't get a period after being on the pill for a while and that's totally normal. I'm sorry, is that TMI?"

He looks so confused right now and maybe even angry. Shit. What have I done?

"*That's* why you haven't returned my calls?"

"I didn't want to talk to you until I knew what to tell you. Until I could tell you everything, and I wanted to do it in person."

"Fudging hell, Ute. There is no TMI when it comes to you and me. Why don't you get that? What do I have to say or do to be the first person you call, no matter what?"

I place the palm of my hand over his heart, and we both lean forward so I can rest my forehead against his. "Is there no untranslatable word for this?"

"There's I love you. I fudging love you, and you aren't allowed to not call me just because you don't know what to say. How's that?"

"Adequate."

He pulls his head back so he can look at my face. "Are you saying you were hoping to be pregnant? With my kid?"

"I'm saying it wouldn't have been terrible if I were. But I'm not."

"Goddammit, Roxy Carter. I would put such an immature entitled ass of a baby in you if you let me."

"But you want a bunch of kids, and I don't know if I can have that many at this point. Is this... Oh God, I guess I have to ask—is this a deal breaker for you?"

He doesn't even hesitate to answer. "Woman. I would

have no problem adopting a kid who wasn't born with my amazing genetic characteristics, but I think the world deserves at least one person with your charming personality and my looks, don't you?"

I nod and take a swig of my beer.

"Are you crying?" he asks.

"I'm processing some emotions in a totally cool and masculine way."

He wipes away the tear and takes my free hand in his. "We deal with everything that we need to deal with together from now on. Get it?"

I nod again. "I get it."

We both turn to look back inside the apartment from the patio. All those happy kids and parents inside. I flash back to the night of the wedding, the two of us out there on the deck while everyone else was inside and how it felt like we were so separate from all that joyful togetherness that was going on without us. But it's not like that anymore.

"Sorry to be the bearer of bad news, but I'm your plus one, Roxy Carter. I'm your emergency contact. I'm your everything. And one of these days, I'm going to be your husband and the father of your child or children. So get used to it. And you know what—fuck it—now that we're on the subject..." He pulls a small velvet box from the pocket of his blazer. "Get used to wearing this."

He flips open the box and presents me with a stunning platinum ring with a light-blue jewel in the center. It matches the color of my irises almost exactly, glinting in the sunlight spectacularly.

"What is that—aquamarine?"

"It's a blue diamond, dummy. They're very rare."

I can't even speak. That thing must be three carats. I don't even want to know how many hundreds of thousands of dollars it's worth.

"It was my grandmother's engagement ring. When she passed, my grandfather gave it directly to me because he didn't trust my mother to ever part with it when the time came. I've been keeping it in a safe at a bank for a few years. I went to get it this morning."

I gulp and carefully place my bottle on the ground, so I don't spill beer on that thing.

"How perfect is it for you? Ice blue. My new favorite color."

"Keaton. Are you asking me to marry you?"

"No. I'm telling you to marry me."

"Are you out of your motherflorking mind? We haven't even been dating for a month!"

"Really? Because it feels like it's been a mother-florking century."

"Holy Schmidt, Keaton. This is insane. That is the most beautiful ring I have ever seen."

"Then take the damn thing out of my hand, put it on, and marry me."

I cover my mouth with both hands and shake my head before finally reaching for the little box. "Okay, fine. It'll be fine."

"Damn right it will." He gulps down about half his bottle of beer.

"I know that."

"Good."

I grab his stupid handsome face and kiss him. "I love you."

"You ducking better."

"I really do. I'm going to marry you. But I'm not going to wear the ring until after the party's over. So we don't take the attention away from Finn."

He grins at me. "You've got a good heart, Roxy Carter." He holds his hand out for me to return the box to him I snap it shut, close to his fingers, like Richard Gere does to Julia Roberts with the necklace box in *Pretty Woman*. He gets the reference and fakes a big toothy laugh, and then he returns the box to his jacket pocket like it's a pack of gum or something. "I cannot wait to knock you up."

"I cannot wait for you to knock me up." I grab his face to kiss him again, and I may never stop.

We pull away from each other when we hear the patio door slide open and Finn's little voice. "Ewww. Why are you guys kissing?" His face is painted green with one big eye in the center and a huge smiling mouth full of teeth.

"He had something on his mouth," I say. "I was just wiping it off. With my mouth."

Finn wrinkles his nose. That seems to be the only reaction I'm getting from children today. "That's not what you were doing."

"I couldn't breathe, so she was giving me mouth-to-mouth."

"Was not. You guys are gross."

"Oh, buddy," Keaton says. "You have no idea."

"What's going on out here?" Aimee pokes her head out, assesses the situation, and smiles. "All good?"

"It'll be fine," I say as casual as I can be, knowing that I'm engaged and Keaton has a priceless blue diamond ring in his pocket.

Chase pops out behind them. "S'up, guys?"

"Oh, you know," Keaton says, standing up and pulling me up with him. "Just Roxy being Roxy."

He picks up our beers, and we follow the McKays inside.

I get another flash of images and feelings, this time of our whole future life together.

Kids and dogs and friends and family. A wedding with strings of warm white lights, and for once I know for certain who my date will be. Parties and play dates and holidays. Messes and triumphs and untranslatable words and perfect moments of silence. I want it all with this man, and I'm going to give him everything I have to give.

I reach behind myself so he can take my hand. He leans down and whispers in my ear, "We don't have to stay behind to help clean up, do we?"

"Hell no. Nina and Bernadette are on clean-up duty. We're going to your place to have sex in one hour."

He hands me my beer. "Prepare your uterus for greatness, future wife."

"Prepare your penis for battle, future husband." We clink bottles again.

"God, I love you. We're going to break every bed we sleep in."

EPILOGUE - KEATON

Two Years Later

"I t's a square!" Bernie yells out. "*WALL-E!*"

"How do you get *WALL-E* from a square?" Matt mutters, thoroughly amused by her.

"He has a square body!"

"Oh my gosh, draw faster!" their daughter Harriet blurts out.

Finn ignores them and continues carefully drawing another square on the upright dry erase board while the sand from the one-minute hourglass falls.

"It's a TV!" Vince offers. "*Poltergeist!*"

"That's not a family movie!" Nina hisses from across the room.

"It's about a family! It's fun!"

"Is that a book?" Harriet jumps up. "*The Jungle Book!*

Harry Potter! The Secret Garden! Alice in Wonderland! Nancy Drew!"

Finn keeps shaking his head and frowning at Harriet.

"*Charlie and the Chocolate Factory!* Draw something else! Something different! Oh my God, is anyone going to help me out?"

"It's a recipe book!" Graziella McKay shouts. "*Ratatouille!*"

"If it was *Ratatouille,* he'd draw a rat." Sean nudges his wife.

"You don't know this! He's a clever boy!"

"Oh, it's a box! *WALL-E!*" Bernie covers her husband's mouth before he can make fun of her. "I love that movie."

Finn signals for them to keep going.

"Is it a toy box?" Harriet squeals. "*Toy Story! Toy Story Two!* Oh no, is it *Toy Story Three?* That one's sad!"

Finn keeps shaking his head and signaling to keep going.

"It's a boxing movie!" Sean yells out. "*Rocky!*"

Chase slowly turns his head to look at me. I slowly turn my head to look at Roxy. She blatantly ignores us and tries to keep her eyes glued to the dry erase board, where Finn decides to start drawing a happy face and then an arrow pointing from the head to the box.

"Time!" Nina calls out.

"It better not be *Seven,*" Chase grumbles.

"It was *Seven!*"

"*Seven?*" Harriet throws her hands up in the air. "That's not a movie!"

"It's not a kids' movie, that's for sure." Aimee gives

Roxy and me the stink eye. "Who put that title in the basket?"

"I did!" Finn says.

Chase and Aimee glare at me.

"We have not let him watch it yet—tell 'em, Finnegan!"

"I haven't seen it yet. I just know there's a head in a box, and I really want to see it!"

"Seven? That's a number!" Harriet's fists are on her hips. It's her most common stance whenever she's talking to Finn now. "You're supposed to make it easy for us so our team can win! Why didn't you just go like this?" She swipes the pen from him and makes seven slashes on the board. "You're seven years old! Joni's seven! I'm seven! You could have just pointed at me!"

Finn erases everything on the board. "Why would I point at you? The title wasn't *Smelly Poopie Head Who Thinks She Knows Everything and Talks Too Much!*"

Chase and Matt exchange looks. Bernie and Aimee exchange looks. We are all aware that one day the McKays and the McGoverns may be related by marriage. I can't wait to have a man-to-man talk with my godson one day about the pros and cons—but mostly pros—of marrying a beautiful mouthy lady who makes your blood boil.

I lock eyes with my lovely wife.

Roxy fudging Bridges.

We've enjoyed a number of beers together outside on sunny days, and she has made good on her promise to never stop telling me that she loves me. Even when those three words are surrounded by a string of words that would make a weaker man cry. So far, I've only cried twice since we got together.

When we got married, three months after getting engaged, and when Roxy gave birth to our baby.

We got pregnant *two* months after getting engaged.

Oops.

Cassie Reyna Bridges is one year old today, which is why we're having a low-key get-together at our house with the crew. I'm putting Joe and Melinda Carter up at a hotel while they stay in town for a few days. My parents couldn't make it tonight because they're traveling Europe, but that's okay. Chase's parents are here.

Cassie's currently taking a nap in the baby carrier I'm wearing. She's basically walking now, but I still like to attach her to my chest whenever she'll let me. I know *I* smell amazing, and I know all newborn heads smell good, but I swear they should make a candle that smells like this kid's skull. That enticing baby fresh scent never went away. It's my personal belief that her brain emits a delicious odor because it's filled with brilliant, sweet, and spicy thoughts.

She has my beautiful brown eyes, my former nanny's calm demeanor, and my wife's beautiful, bossy loud mouth.

We're expecting to one day nickname her Sassy Cassie, but lately it has been Gassy Cassie, to our great misfortune. Seriously, she's as explosive as her parents' chemistry. We're working on getting her to talk less while she's eating. She mostly says "Ja-po!" over and over while cramming food into the general area of her mouth and pointing at the dog, who follows her everywhere. Roxy assumes she's saying Jackpot, but it's obvious to me that she's trying to say "Keaton." Maybe even "asshole," which is what her mommy calls me every now and then when she forgets my name. Hormones and all that.

In a few years, Cassie will be going to the same preschool as Franny McKay, Edward "Don't Call Him Eddie" McGovern, and Davina Devlin. There are currently four strollers in our house. There was definitely something in the water over there in Antigua. And Indiana. We all spent so much time at the maternity ward over a three-month period that the nurses started calling us The Mat Pack. "Mat" was supposedly short for maternity, but I think they all had a crush on McGovern. Whatever. They'll all be on Team Keaton by the end of the summer.

Cassie will always be surrounded by her best friends, and so will we.

One plus one equals infinity.

After the uproar about *Seven* finally dies down, Roxy gets up to pick out a kids' movie title. Her baby bump has started to show, and I think all of her life-giving curves are the sexiest thing ever. She's due again in less than five months, and we're so excited to be having a boy that she's almost forgiven me for knocking her up sooner than we had planned. What can I say? My sperm is very seductive and also, I couldn't wait to see if her boobs will get even bigger this time. For scientific reasons.

She bends forward to pick out a piece of paper from the basket on the coffee table, giving me a private glimpse of her magnificent cleavage, bless her heart.

One second after glancing at the paper, she nods her

head and steps over to the dry erase board, picks up the pen, and nods at Vince to flip over the hourglass.

She draws a leg with a foot, and I know immediately that it's: "*The LEGO Movie.*"

"Yes!"

"There's a movie about LEGOs?" my father-in-law asks. "People paid to see that?"

Roxy is already erasing the leg and drawing a balloon.

"It's a balloon!" Joni yells out. "*Up!*"

Roxy draws a line into the balloon and then draws a squiggly, deflated balloon.

"*Mary Poppins,*" I say.

"Yes!"

"What? How'd you get that?" Joni stares at me, wide-eyed.

"It's a popped balloon," Nina explains for me. "Smart."

"Oh, is it *The Red Balloon?*" Melinda exclaims.

"It was *Mary Poppins.*" Joe pats her on the knee.

"I love this movie, *The Red Balloon,*" Graziella leans over to say to Melinda. "They don't make movies like this anymore."

Roxy is on to the next one, drawing a face with big eyes and a round, open mouth.

"*Monsters, Inc!*" Nina and Joni yell at the same time.

I already know what the movie is before Roxy finishes drawing the hands on the boy's face, but I'll let someone else guess first. We don't have to prove to anyone how well we know each other anymore.

"Is it that cartoon car movie?" Joe asks.

"That's not a car," his wife elbows him. "Dummy."

As soon as Roxy starts to draw the outline of a Christmas tree behind the boy, Joni shouts out, "*Home Alone!*"

"Yes!"

Nina high-fives Joni, and they do a little jig while taunting Vince. "We're beating you!"

Roxy starts to draw something that is clearly an animal with four legs and might be a dog.

"Is that a dog? *Lady and the Tramp!*" Melinda says.

"*Lady and the Tramp,* she'd draw two dogs," her husband mutters.

"Oh hush, you."

"*Hotel for Dogs!*" Joni squeals.

"*Beethoven. The Shaggy Dog. The Shaggy D.A,. Bolt, Marley & Me, My Dog Skip,* the one with Richard Gere!" Nina knows a lot of dog movies.

Roxy shakes her head while drawing something on the underside of the animal. Possibly a penis. Or an udder.

"*Mulan,*" I say, grinning.

Vince calls, "Time!"

"Yes! Four points!" She comes over to me, and we give each other a very delicate high-five so we don't wake our sleeping toddler.

"What? How'd you get *Mulan* from that?" Finn scratches his head, dramatically.

"A cow goes moo," I say, as if it's obvious.

"A cow goes moo," she whispers, kissing Cassie on the top of her head while rubbing her own belly.

I get you, Roxy Bridges.

I fudging love every single person in this house right

THE PLUS ONES   281

now, but I cannot wait to be alone with my girls and
my dog.

Bedtime is the best time of day, every day, right after
mornings and dinner.

But only when Roxy doesn't snore.

We still haven't broken the custom-made bed.

But we're working on it.

We'll never stop trying.

#ROXTON4EVA

THE END

AUTHOR'S NOTE

1. If you have not already read my other Brooklyn/NYC books, you will find Chase and Aimee's story in *Tonight You're Mine* (where Keaton is an ass); Matt and Bernadette's story in *Come Back to Bed*; Vince and Nina's story in *Rebound with Me*.

2. There is a wonderful little coffee table book called *LOST IN TRANSLATION: An Illustrated Compendium of Untranslatable Words from Around the World* by Ella Frances Sanders. Not all of Keaton's untranslatable words are in here, but most are. It's a sweet little book.

3. The word that Keaton didn't know how to pronounce is: *Mamihlapinatapei*. According to Wikipedia, it is listed in the *GUINNESS BOOK OF WORLD RECORDS* as The Most Succinct Word. A Yaghan noun, defined in the book *LOST IN TRANSLATION* as: A silent acknowledgement and understanding between two people, who

are both wishing or thinking the same thing (and are both unwilling to initiate).

4. The Coco Beach Resort in Antigua is inspired by this gorgeous corner of the internet: http://www.cocoshotel.com/ If you go there, send me pics!

Made in the USA
Coppell, TX
14 November 2023

24191764R00173